# Women Who Write With Elves

## An Anthology

Cover Art by C.A. Speakman
Photography Credit: Crystal Graphics

Women Who Write With Elves are Annis Farnell, Elves, Enza Vynn-Cara, Julia Chalkley, Mairibeth MacMillan, Palo Stickland, R Cohen, RJ Ashby and Sue Cook.

Women Who Write With Elves is a group of nine writers who met through the Open University. Scattered from Scotland to Switzerland, we keep in touch via an online forum.

Once a year we meet for a creative writing break which is stimulating, educational and far from the relaxing holiday some of us hope for! Our inaugural meeting was on the Isle of Tiree in the Inner Hebrides. It was a perfect writers' retreat — isolated, beautiful, windswept and, best of all, free.

Members include published novelists, poets and short story writers who have gained success in competitions and national magazines. Our name reflects that we are all women except for one lone gentleman — the eponymous Mr Elves. His claim to be the descendant of a Portuguese pirate has earned him the roles of volunteer galley slave and...editor.

# Contents

## A Glass, Half Empty

*Elves*

Spring holds such promise,
potential of a new year.
But storms threaten.

Summer sun, warm days.
holiday, beside the sea.
Cannot last forever.

Autumn harvest festival,
fruit, corn, barley.
But Winter approaches.

Winter white, cold days,
white berries, snow and Jack Frost.
Central heating bills.

## A Good Marriage

*Palo Stickland*

Looking in the same direction
the picture on a Christmas card
summed it up, perfectly.

I thought, yes
that's it.
A vision of togetherness,
two people hugging close.
On her arm,
a basket laden with food.
On his, a tree.

Looking in the same direction,
they gaze at the town square.
At the carol singers in full voice,
at skaters on the lake

I thought, no
the vision fades.

You are gone.
I search for a reason why
we stopped
looking in the same direction.

## A Perfect Fit

*Enza Vynn-Cara*

The slender foot swung back and forth. The toes pointed and slid in between the leather straps and the sole. A delicate hand pulled the back sling into place, secured the side buckle, and then tapped the tanned skin from the calf to the bend of the knee.

'Delicious,' Mr Cerutti observed.

'I'm not sure.' Mrs Leyton rotated, flexed, arched, and then thrust her foot forward, piercing the air in front of Mr Cerutti's crotch. 'It hasn't got the feel I want.' She thumped the chunky heel on the chequered floor, lifted and thrust the foot forward again. 'Nah, it just doesn't. It feels tight.'

'Mrs Leyton, a moment please.' Mr Cerutti caught the foot in mid-air with both his hands. The whiff of what he called 'a long summer walk' rose out of Mrs Leyton's slightly damp foot and clashed with the Chanel Number 5 he was sure she must have bathed in. He stared at Mrs Leyton's right knee, which was round and smooth and had a small raised mole that reminded him of a beetle. Slowly, he let his gaze ascend the scooped neckline of her red summer dress to rest on the woman's round face, creaseless but for tiny ripples at the corners of her Mona Lisa smile.

'May I try something?' he asked.

'If you must.'

The woman lifted the hem of her dress higher than Mr Cerutti had intended. Wanting to return the smile she offered but thinking it best to focus on the job ahead, he lowered his gaze to what he believed was Mrs Leyton's best asset after her smile: the slender calf, the slim and perfectly arched plant, the mildly sloped edge of her toes. 'You know, it's actually a very good fit. The foot must be one with the shoe and that is a tricky thing to get. I feel these sandals far outweigh the ones your husband chose last week. And I know that you wanted these all along. Your foot is shaped for this type of shoe, Mrs Leyton. See how your toes peek out from beneath the strap, and how your heel doesn't border out in the back?'

'Yes, but Henry won't like them.'

'How could one not see the perfect ensemble of your rather petite and perfectly arched foot, the slender red and black leather sandal, the chunky heel and gold rim?'

'He thinks red is trashy.'

'Nonsense, Mrs Leyton. Red is Valentino.'

Mr Cerutti forced a cough to hide the irritation crawling up his throat. The Wall Street oriented and impeccably dressed Mr Leyton couldn't possibly appreciate such a combination. The man might as well be colour-blind. The few times he had accompanied his wife, he looked lost yet resolute in his assumption that colour did not belong on his wife's feet. All shades from pure white to natural black were the gold standard to any woman's sensible dress code and he proceeded to let Mr Cerutti in on this by snorting and letting his thick glasses slide down an aquiline nose whenever he stooped to inspect any non-greyscale shoe.

He was never pleased, always finding something wrong with Mrs Leyton's feet as with the shoe itself: too long for the big toe, too harsh around the calf, too much space around the much too fat Achilles' heel. The poor woman ended up buying the one he suggested or another just as grey and dull — pump without circumstance. A sore sight, each time it happened, and Mr Cerutti couldn't bring himself to seal the deal, leaving the task of swiping and rendering back Mr Leyton's plastic card to his assistants.

Having Mrs Leyton's feet all to himself was a rarity he aimed to decorate as he pleased.

Red.

'You see Mrs Leyton, your lovely foot is like this sandal. It must tenderly be prepared to fit. Now, if you allow me. May I?'

'Of course, Mr Cerutti.'

Mrs Leyton toned down her usually high pitch to a husky whisper, which Mr Cerutti was more than willing to please. He slid the sandal off, stretched the Italian leather straps, the front and the back, and toyed with the flexibility of the sole. Then, after a small pause, he wrapped his hand around the back of her ankle, rested the heel of her foot on his knee and took a deep breath.

Another whiff of summer walk, and not enough Chanel Number 5, flooded his nostrils and he could not hold back a sudden sneeze. Hardly the proper thing to do. It would disarray his professional pitch, fine-tuned by years of practice, and reserved only for his most faithful customers. Besides, Mrs Leyton's foot odour was of the milder kind and he rather enjoyed it. Yes, he thought, as he gazed at her, truly enjoyable.

Faking a cough to hide the unwanted sneeze, Mr Cerutti took another deep breath and forced his senses to follow the trail of Coco Chanel — not Number 5 as he had first thought. He said, 'What we need is a massage to get the circulation going. First some strokes towards the ankle like this, then around the heel and back to the toes, which, may I add, are perfectly shaped.'

'Ah yes.' The woman whispered through peach coloured lips. 'But Mr Leyton is of the opposite idea.'

'Feet are not hedge funds,' Mr Cerutti said, noting how his client's lips curved into another Mona Lisa smile. 'Now if you please, a light rotation clockwise.'

'Like this?'

Mr Cerutti nodded. 'Then a wider rotation anti-clockwise.'

'Like this?'

'Yes, yes, now let me flex and extend it for you, first upward, then downward. Up. Down. Up and down.'

'Ah...' Mrs Leyton closed her eyes as her cheeks tinged pink and red, which pleased even more Mr Cerutti.

'Yes, now it comes. Relax.' His slim hand reached blindly for the sandal and aimed it at Mrs Leyton's foot. 'Now stretch those toes,' he urged, his hand guiding the back of her heel.

'Get them into the strapped tunnel. There you are.'

'It's tight,' the woman whined, easing back into a halo of sunlight reflecting off the mirror behind her.

'Patience, Mrs, Leyton. A little wiggle and then a push.' Mr Cerutti shut his eyes and wrapped his hands around the woman's ankle. 'There, now a tad to the right, and to the left. Feel the stretch? And how the tightness gives way?'

'Oh yeah.'

'Now ease out and thrust it in again, deeper, deeper. Wiggle, wiggle, deep thrust and... Hold.' Mr Cerutti opened his eyes, stared at the woman's flushed face. 'How does it feel now, Mrs Leyton?'

'Oh, Mr Cerutti. It fits, it fits.'

## Bargain

*Julia Chalkley*

As soon as Dave saw the entrance fee he knew his visit to the Hedingham Craft Fair had been a bad idea. Two pounds, just to come into the village hall and spend money! But he had no choice. He paid up and joined the slow motion conga, shuffling forward at the rate of one step a second to get into the hall where the Tannoy was belting out fruity carols and the stallholders lurked like vampires. He'd messed up properly this year and he knew it. He had to get Christmas sorted, and fast.

Same for everyone else in the hall, by the look of it. Hands reached out to grab at items on the trestle tables before anyone else spotted the bargain and snatched it away — greyish carved soap dolls in fuchsia pink gingham dresses, dented tin tree decorations covered in hastily painted holly leaves and small greasy cupcakes that disintegrated as they were picked up. The buyers were thrusting money at the stallholders and snatching the change from their hands.

Christmas Eve. Brings out the best in people.

Feeling sick and pressured, Dave stepped out of the mobile queue of people into a clear space in front of a stall and held on to the edge of the table. No one was stopping here, so there was no one jostling for a place and the air felt cooler. As he looked at the goods, he could see why.

Christmas cards. Nice cards, he had to admit. But unless you were handing them over, a little too late. Dave could see the last date for posting Christmas cards shining white on the inside of his eyelids every time he shut his eyes. Twentieth of December. Four days ago. He'd seen the notice in the Post Office this morning when he went in to buy his stamps. The clerk had smirked when he'd asked for Christmas stamps, but hadn't commented.

The woman behind the stall was shining. The blonde of her glossy hair was natural, he'd swear to it, and the smooth pale skin had a subtle texture that was surely not caked in make-up. Her eyes were steady on his. Normally he hated being stared at by people who were trying to sell him something — he always ended up buying whatever it was, even if he didn't want it — but her eyes were something else. A very pale, soft blue. The colour of the sky on a clear winter morning.

Well, he did need cards. He'd post them anyway, with a jokey message wishing his relatives a Happy New Year. It was only after he'd picked out a selection that he noticed the price list by her elbow.

'Five pounds – each?' Dave picked up the list and held it close to his face, looking for the smudge that hid the line about ten cards for a fiver, or something similar. Nope. 'Sophie's Cards', it read. 'Five pounds.'

'That's right,' Sophie said.

'Are they sprinkled with gold dust?'

Sophie laughed, and held out her hand. 'Trust me,' she said. 'These cards are worth the money. They're hand made with love and a sprinkle of fairy dust.'

Dave looked at the cards on the stall again. They had all the stuff on them that people liked, all the holly and angels and tartan ribbon and stuff like that. But nothing else. No glitter, no sparkle, no fairy dust that he could see.

'You have to post these?' Sophie asked.

'Yes… I was going to write some joke in them about getting stuck in the post,' Dave admitted. 'My relatives are used to me sending cards late, but this year's been worse than usual.'

'You don't need to joke,' Sophie said, putting the cards into a small paper sack with a final, sexy stroke across the surface of each as she did so. 'Just wish them a happy Christmas and that's what they'll have. Fifty pounds, please.'

Dave was about to say something rude, but as she smiled at him he smiled back and pulled out his wallet, picking out five tenners and passing them over to her in what felt like slow motion.

'Thank you,' Sophie said, handing over the little paper sack of cards. 'Post them in the box at the end of Holly Lane for the best results.'

'Results?' Dave said, then had to get out of the way of a large man in a coat the colour of cat-sick who was so determined to get to Sophie's stall that he shoved Dave across to the next stall. Dave dodged a woman with a large knobbly walking stick and a nasty glare, and ended up back in the long queue, being prodded and tutted along with the grumbling brook of people past the crumbly cake stall and the rank cheese stall and the dented tin ornament stall. He kept going till he reached the exit and was popped out of the tropical heat of the village hall and into the damp grey High Street.

Dave didn't have the heart to go looking for Christmas presents now. A man who paid fifty quid for a few cards was obviously not competent to be let loose on the shops without a guardian. So he went straight home and sat down with a glass of wine to write out his cards.

He was used to scribbling 'Merry Christmas' in each card, right under the printed line that said 'Merry Christmas'. Years ago he used to struggle to find something original and witty to say, but it had never turned out well. Usually he wrote something that he immediately realised would be read as an insult, and had to add a hasty few lines of explanation and apology. Occasionally he spelt some of the words wrong. Two years ago he'd written what he was thinking, telling his sister that the robins on the card were just like the ones on her knickers. In his defence, she had once owned a pair of knickers with similar robins on, and had insisted on pulling up her skirt to show them to every relative at the family's Christmas party. But that was his sister at five years old. Twenty-six years on, she was unlikely to appreciate the memory. He'd torn up the card and sent her one with 'Merry Christmas, Dave' in it.

This year, his card writing session was different.

The pen nib flowed across the card, leaving behind lines of sharp black words that didn't quite look like his handwriting. The words weren't his, either. 'Merry Christmas' was part of every message, but after that there was a short witty run of words, different each time. After each message was the word 'Dave', looking more like expensive and desirable artwork than a name.

He'd finished the cards, addressed the envelopes and had them all stamped within an hour. And he felt good, too, slightly drunk and grinning. He reached for his wine glass.

It was full.

Dave sat looking at the glass for a while before he picked it up to drink. He hadn't turned to his glass once since he'd sat down to write. That had to be a record.

He felt like testing Sophie's instructions to the full. He stuffed the cards into a carrier bag, got his coat and went out into the drizzle. He passed four post boxes as he headed for Holly Lane with long strides. Just as he turned the corner into Holly Lane, he saw the post van pull away from the post box. Dave realised then that it didn't matter. He'd missed the last post collection before Christmas.

He fed the cards slowly through the slot in the Holly Lane post box. As the last card dropped into the empty cavern, he gripped the edge of the slot, leaning against the cold cast iron face and staring for a long time at the chipped red paint on the embossed 'E II R'. He felt cold and very miserable. He'd have to apologise for this, he knew it. Again. This time, his family were just not going to accept a simple sorry.

The following morning, the phone was ringing through his dreams for a minute or two before he surfaced. Dave grabbed the handset and almost dropped it. Even with the phone held a foot away from his ear, he could hear his sister's voice yelling.

'Merry Christmas!'

'Angie…' Dave sat up in bed. 'And happy Christmas to you too!'

God, she never sounded this cheerful at Christmas. She was always yelling at her kids to clear up their toys, or slamming the turkey down on the kitchen worktop and shouting at Keith to bloody well carve it.

'You are coming over?' Angie said.

'Sure, about midday?'

Angie snorted. 'Now, idiot! Come on, there's a bottle of champagne with your name on it. Come and get your present, it's lurking under our tree like some giant panda.'

'I haven't got you anything…'

'Oh, don't worry about that,' Angie said.

Something in her tone was odd. She meant it. She was happy. She couldn't give a Paxo's stuff about Dave's present, or lack of.

In for a penny… 'And I reckon your card will arrive just before the end of January,' Dave said.

He heard her laugh at the other end of the phone. Laugh! Angie! 'Yeah, so funny. Yours was one of the first to arrive. God, we panicked when we saw it, got us to sit down and do ours. How did you do it?'

'Do what?' Dave asked. Posted the cards in the Holly Lane post box, but how …

'I mean, what you wrote in your card. I'd had such a lousy day, and seeing your card on the doormat - yours is always the last card through the letterbox, so I thought if your card's arrived I'm well behind. And then …'

Angie laughed again. Extraordinary. 'You know what? When I got to the end of your limerick …' Limerick! Dave thought. Did I write a limerick in her card? '… Well,' Angie said, 'I just felt … it was going to be a happy Christmas. And I woke up this morning thinking I had to fetch you over here early and we'd have a proper family Christmas together. Come over now. You can open your present with ours, then we can shut the kids in the living room to make a racket with their presents and get stuck into the hard stuff in the kitchen.'

Dave said Yes, and Sure, and Goodbye, and had put the phone down before he could work out whether Angie was joking or not.

After he'd rung his parents, three of his aunts and his cousin, Dave had a mystery on his hands. All of his cards had arrived. What's more, they'd all arrived three weeks ago. Not one relative had sounded as if they were being sarcastic, or senile, or joking. And they were all, in their own ways, happy.

'Five pounds each,' Dave said to himself.

He got dressed and found his keys before adding quietly, 'Bargain.'

## Context

*RJ Ashby*

Female adolescence is – universally – an emotionally and psychologically intense period. (Caitlin Flanagan)

Seventeen year old Rhea was finished with school, done with adolescent boys and on leave. She was at her zenith.

Today the sea was not so blue anymore. It remonstrated with violent spray from acres of anger and chaos. The air tasted of salt. The rain too, as it lashed the walls of the nearest cottage that had cowered below the headland for two hundred years. Smoke was sucked from the chimney and strewn inland. Rhea loved days like this. For as long as she could remember she loved the isolation of weather, of this place. Family holidays secreted away on the coast, way, way up north. Rhea owned this trip. She and Sylvja, a school friend, planned hedonistic indulgence… day into night into day… no parents… no rules. And no more Bill!

She rose early. She had plans but the rain had doused them. The flames licked up the side of the logs, a crackle spat red then black and a puff of wood-smoke ducked out. A warm glow of gold from the pine panelled walls washed by artificial lights replaced the lacking sun. Rhea padded in her baggy socks from the kitchen back to the fire. The rumble from the kettle stopped her from settling just yet.

The house was just the way it had been built in eighteen hundred and something, now remodelled. Two cottages – together now – not exactly grand designs.

Rhea settled on the sagging sofa, a book in hand and a cup of steaming tea. A single tap on the window, a shadow passed and she stiffened. *That* was Bill! She had guessed he would be there too. He had always been there but now she had cast him off.

'Please… don't come in!' she whispered.

She knew he wouldn't. Not after her wrath. She stole through to the kitchen and watched the flop of his mousey hair as he ran through the marram grass to the beach below. Last year she would have followed... Was his hair longer? Had he grown? She watched, remembering...

'Come on!' he had shouted to her, egging her on, and day by day she had swum further and further from the shore. Goggled and flippered they had crossed the bay. Her confidence had grown. Wild swimming he had called it.

She flew to the upstairs window. Soon the dark head of her rejected lover bobbed into view and he swam out into the buffeting waves. Memories held her — she only saw last year's sand, last year's sun, last year's … love. It had looked like love… only because they were isolated here, only because their families were friends, only because he was there. She was better than him. He was a geek, a beanpole, acne pitted and… She remembered her compliance. How could she have let him? The cave had hidden their tentative groping, their secret lovemaking. She shuddered. No one could ever know.

Then he had found her in Edinburgh! At school! She cringed. He was waiting for her. He stood by the school gates with a lone red rose. A grin lit his face.

'Fuck off, you moron!' She had spat back.

Now in the living room Rhea tried to lose herself in a story of real love.

'There's some idiot out there swimming, Rhea. I've never seen rain like it. Some place this. Don't tell me that this is it!' Sylvja hesitated on the stairs. Her glistening high heels below skinny jeans were out of place. She flipped her designer handbag over her shoulder and sashayed to the sofa.

'Oh don't mind the rain. There's always one day like this. It's a price you have to pay for a holiday in Scotland.'

'I can't get a signal on my phone? I had it on charge all night.' She groaned.

'Some networks don't get a signal. You can use my phone if you need.'

'Need? I need mine! And now! How can I manage without it! Wi-Fi?'

'No sorry.'

'OMG. Are you serious?' She frowned.

'The pub. You can get it at the pub, or the hotel.'

'So — what with the rain — no phone — no computer — how long are we staying? What a godforsaken place Rhea! Pub — how bloody far is that?'

'It's about a mile. Let's stay in today — reading, games, DVDs, drawing. Oh and cooking. We can have pancakes if you like.' Sylvja rolled her eyes.

'So who is the swimmer?' Sylvja asked later. She was settled in front of the fire painting her nails.

'Oh — the neighbour. William McMenemy.'

'A friend?'

'He's an idiot — a nerd. He stays with his mother, here, in the summer. He's a 'scheme-y' from Edinburgh. Lives with his dad.'

'I thought you would die if you swam in the sea up here!' Sylvja was serious.

'No. You wear a wetsuit.' She laughed.

'Have you got one?'

'Yes.'

'So you swim too? In the bay? Don't expect me! Look.' She held her nails out for inspection. 'Any good films?'

By the next morning the weather had lost its violence. Sylvja sat on the garden wall, her face to the sun. 'You taking a picnic too?'

'Yes. Can you carry those seats? I've got the rest. Get something to read!'

'We need help. Is that guy around?'

Bill was on the headland above them. He lay on the grass, warming in the sun after his swim, his wetsuit draped on an outcrop of rock. Below the rocks the white sand glistened, smooth, unspoilt.

He saw the blonde as she tottered. He saw her dark glasses, her sunhat and her short summer dress. He saw she was struggling to carry two folding chairs, an Ikea bag and her handbag.

He skipped down to help.

'Here, can I take something?' He dropped in by Sylvja.

'Oh you are a darling. Thanks.' She turned her full smile on him and dropped her awkward bundles. 'I'm Sylvja. You know Rhea?' She pointed to the distant figure.

'Yes. I sure do.' He carried the seats all the way to the beach. He put them down by Rhea and nodded to them both. 'Catch you later.' And he jogged off along the beach, towards the village. 'Need anything from the shops, Rhea?' He called back.

'No!' she shouted back, irritated, adding a whispered 'Shit face!' as an afterthought.

He smiled, waved and then continued along the beach.

'Don't encourage him, Sylvja. I mean it. Ignore him. He's stalking us.'

'Whatever!'

Rhea changed into her wetsuit. She carried her flippers and goggles to the shoreline. She swam out into the bay, then turned onto her back to enjoy her daring.

Sylvja stripped to her bikini and lay. When a squeal echoed across the bay, she squinted in that direction. She saw a group in the sea at the far end. Each had a surfboard. Parked on the sand was an old black Land Rover. Rhea was still bobbing in the middle distance.

Sylvja sauntered off to investigate. She wandered along the edge of the sea, sometimes she let the cold water pool round her ankles, other times she skipped and danced to avoid it. She watched the boys. Some skimmed effortless ahead of the waves, others floundered and splattered into the deep. Eventually she stood, an observer of their prowess. One by one the surfers glided ever closer to her. Then they were on the shore, intrigued and interested — they in their black glistening skins, she in golden near-nakedness with her blonde hair free.

In time the boys returned to sport with the sea and she retraced her steps, dancing with the flowing tide. Bill caught up with her for a bit before he took a path off through the dunes.

Sylvja called out to Rhea. 'Hi, Rhea. Beach party tonight. Those guys along there.' She pointed.

'What — Gavin?' Rhea tried to keep her tone even.

'Is he the blonde one? The cool dude.'

‘The one with the Land Rover.’ Rhea had never been invited to a beach party. She and Bill had dug into the dying embers of a bonfire, the morning after. Once they found a bottle of wine, unopened.

‘Hey that guy, that Bill guy. He’s ok. He’s going to Oxford. He says I can use his computer – any time.’

Rhea lying on her back grunted. ‘Mmm.’ She snoozed. Oxford was a surprise. She hadn’t thought he was that clever!

The beach was greying in the evening light but the sun still shone. It would bleed red across the sea before it sank out of sight. On the far side of the beach there was a huddle and smoke and the flickering flames from a camp fire. Music drifted out over the sea, a mercury mirror. Rhea and Sylvja’s black figures moved across the beach. Laughter rippled out to them. The air was electric.

‘Hi girls. Sylvja – see I remembered – with a ‘j’. Drink?’ Gavin held out beer. The girls stood, the heat of the fire on their faces, grinning. Other lads hovered. Sylvja took Gavin’s jacket and put it round her own shoulders. Laughter rallied between them. Other girls sat back. Couples sat close. The sun dipped, rinsing them all in blood before it too died. Someone was playing a guitar and there was singing and dancing. Gavin held Sylvja close.

The guys were drinking hard — and swaggering. Rhea sipped her bottle. Two guys were sledging down the dunes screaming through sand clouds. Across the fire Rhea noticed Bill — with a girl. His hair hung thick, bleached from the sun, and uncombed. He looked just like the others. He fitted in.

'Hey bring your Rhea here!' One of the boys was patting the sand and beckoning to her — proud of his joke.

'Rhea, what kind of a name is that?' Another guy had designs on her. He smooched close holding his arm out, offering. Rhea stepped back.

'Hey, hey watch out!'

She had kicked over a bottle of wine. An inebriated youth, perched on a chunk of wood, had caught it before much had dribbled into the sand. He clutched at the bottle.

'Sorry.' She moved in beside him and sat down. He was too drunk to be a threat. She glowered through the dark at her friend. Sylvja had stolen the prize: Gavin.

Rhea's eyes blazed.

She sat, huddled — tomorrow — ruined too. She reached for her phone.

**Mum.**

**Come and get us.**

**It's a nightmare**

**S. is drunk again. R X**

## Crossing the River

*Annis Farnell*

The lands of the Gododdin were guarded to the north by the wide waters of Forth, to the east, by the sharp chop of the North Sea, to the south, the massive wall the Romans had built marked their bounds. In the west, the great fort of Marchidun towered high over the two deep rivers that protected its flanks. From its ramparts, Arthur could see below him the brood mares, the foals and the hay meadows. He turned, surveying his care: the township of Calchvyndd, and beyond to the rolling lands of the Merse; to his left, the rising hills with their tree-clad slopes; to his right, the Tywi's waters surged towards him. He turned again, facing the west, the far peaks of the Eildon Hills, and the Taw running from the far distance, deep in Selgovae territory. This way would come their enemies, but so would their friends.

*Friends,* Arthur thought. *In war, maybe. In peace?* He shook his head, trying to dislodge the uncomfortable thoughts. *When elder leaves are the size of a mouse's ear, women are in season.* And they had been there, at Alcluid, in the spring of the year before. And now, a year later, Gwenddydd, his Gwenddydd, was nursing another man's brat at her blue-veined breast. His fists clenched. As a Celt, he recognised the importance of women, their right to take lovers, especially at Imbolc; as a Christian, he deplored its immorality; as a man, jealousy ruled his waking and sleeping.

'Father!' Ceol, his eldest, ran up excitedly. 'There they come!'

There they came, indeed. His jaw set tight. *I am the Guledig, the Leader of Battles; somehow, I will make them pay.*

Marchidun was large, but the influx of allies made it seem small and cramped. Gwenddydd, as befitted the Guledig's wife, had marshalled her women with as much skill as Arthur ordered his battle line, and soon the timbers of the great hall were thundering with the noise of nine hundred men feasting. At the top table, Arthur sat between Nudus and Dumnogenus, the Princes of Rheged. Gwenddydd let go the anxious breath she had been unconsciously holding. *After all,* she thought, *he forgave me, and accepted the child; he will not risk the battle for a matter of pride.*

Arthur's eyes, darkly blue, met hers over the head of Dumnogenus, and the colour left her face. Here was neither forgiveness nor acceptance, only implacable determination.

Later, in their chamber, she asked, 'What are you going to do?'

He laughed, a jeering, fleering burst of harshness.

'Why do you need to know? So you can betray me again? What sort of a fool do you take me for, woman?'

And would have turned away, but he lusted for her yet, and the elder leaves were as big as a mouse's ear again, and next day, he would lead his army into battle. And perhaps … his death she could contemplate with equanimity, sometimes she felt the burden of being the Guledig's wife too great, but *dear God,* she prayed, *let him not be maimed. Arthur hale is hard enough for any woman to live with.*

In the morning, the fortress looked even more like a broken anthill. Men sharpened swords and spear-points, burnished the fish-scales of mailcoats, checked harness for wear, bustled about, looking busy. Women packed food bags, filled medicine bags with salves and bandages. Horses neighed and stamped, snorted and whinnied and kicked, and dogs and children seemed to be everywhere underfoot, silly with excitement. Trumpeters tried the tone of their instruments, and the dragon banners of the Cymru clapped and flaunted in the stiff breeze.

Coel rode up to the hall door astride Llamrei, Arthur's grey mare.

'Look, Father, I harnessed her myself!' he cried, sliding down from her back.

'Did you so? And did you check the girth?'

'Of course,' the boy replied, affronted.

'Then you can say you had a hand in the battle,' Arthur replied gravely, blue eyes twinkling.

'Can I? But … tacking up a horse is not fighting a battle!'

'How do you think the battle would go, with the Guledig on his arse in the mud? The small things are important too, and so, worth doing well.'

Coel grinned. 'I checked the girth. The Guledig's safe seat is his own affair, now.' And ducked the playful smack the man aimed at his head.

Gwenddydd appeared in the doorway. She carried her husband's weapons, his shield, his six foot contus, the Roman cavalry lance. Aeddan, their second son, gravely handed up the polished helmet with its protective tail — and cheek-plates. Arthur took the sword, and slung it over head and shoulder to hang on his left hip. Little Teneu, their daughter, carried his cloak, and now she lifted it as high as her four-year-old arms could stretch. He kissed her as he bent to take it, and flung its folds around them both for a moment before rising, fastening it with a great gold brooch. Lightly he vaulted into the saddle, with its four horns to hold the rider secure in battle, and reached down for spear and shield. The scarlet cloak, symbol since the days of Paternus Pesrut of the Guledig's authority, settled round him. Behind him, the Rheged princes mounted up, and the trumpeters' bronze carnyxes sounded their brazen summons.

Up Tawside they rode, three alae in loose formation, just as the Romans had taught their forefathers, all easy in their saddles, yet watchful. Scouts ranged ahead of the army, but Arthur was confident of his enemies' next move: the Selgovae and their Pictish allies would sweep down from the heights above Garw, and advance along the level valley bottom. And there, at the confluence of Garw and Annan, where the south bank rose steep and high, they would be forced to cross the lesser water.

The army of horsemen crossed to the north bank of Iekti's stream, driving deep into

Selgovan territory. That the valley was empty spoke for itself: the people had gone, decamped to Garw, the men to answer the call to arms, the women and children to shelter.

The light was fading as they pressed on, until at last, Arthur called a halt. The stocky ponies they rode were tired, but not exhausted, and the short break to rest and eat before dawn would revive horses and men both.

'Every third man to sleep for an hour,' Arthur instructed his second-in-command, Gaullac. 'And the next third in an hour, then the next. Your men, too, my lords,' he ordered the Rheged princes.

In relays, the horses were taken to the river behind them to drink, and allowed to graze. Men slept in their cloaks, or ate bread and meat; there were no fires, no talking.

An hour before dawn, Arthur rode down to Annan. The bank was open, but a little way back along its length, the forest clung to the hillside.

'Gaullac!'

'Guledig?'

'Our men here, in the centre. Prince Dumnogenus!'

'Guledig?'

'The right is yours. And the left to you, Prince Nudus.' The dark blue eyes were hooded in the soft light, Arthur's expression difficult to read.

Nudus thought, *Is it deliberate, giving me the dangerous wing? But someone has to take it, after all.* Nudus nodded, and turned away to draw up his men.

Arthur stopped him.

'You know what is to be done?'

The Rheged nodded.

'I charge on your signal, then hold them at the ford.'

'And you, Dumnogenus?'

'I charge on the second signal, but swing wide and come in on their left.'

'Good. And we will feast in Marchidun tomorrow!' *Unless the corbies are feasting on you...*

'They're coming,' Gaullac said, peering through the screen of leaves.

Dust, and sun sparking off spear-points, and the thunder and grumble of feet and hooves and wheels.

'They've got chariots,' someone said.

'They're Picts, what d'you expect?' retorted another.

‘There's a lot more of them than there are of us.’ This from the inevitable doom-sayer.

‘All the more for Dinter here.’ Arthur grinned, wolfishly, patting his sword-hilt.

The Selgovan army reached the ford, forced together by the trees, by the slope, by the narrow entry to the water.

‘Are they blind?’ Gaullac wondered. ‘Surely they can see us by now.’

‘Not if we’re still. And quiet,’ Arthur added, pointedly.

The trumpeter spat, and raised his carnyx to his lips.

‘Not yet,’ Arthur ordered. Then, quietly still, ‘Loose the dragons!’ and the red and white banners with their dragon heads on tall poles unfurled, and hung drooping.

The Selgovan army was splashing through the water, already two lines forming on the bank. Arthur raised his arm, clutching his spear. The Cymru held its collective breath.

‘Now!’ The order came softly, though no less forceful for that. The spear arm slashed down, pointing to the enemy. And the brazen carnyx belled its challenge, and Prince Nudus’ ala clattered out of hiding; out onto the short spring grass, to the trot, to the canter, and crashed headlong into the startled Selgovans' right wing.

Again the carnyx brayed, and Dumnogenus charged forth, heading away to the enemy's left. A third time it sounded, and Arthur, the Leader of Battles, burst out of his ambush, the dragon heads screaming as the air rushed over the reeds in their mouths, his three hundred in tight, disciplined blocks, surging to smash the enemy centre. It was an old and proven tactic, and it worked again; the Selgovans, on foot, struggling out of the water, chaotic and undisciplined, however ferocious, crumbled before the horsemen's fury. They fled, and were annihilated.

To left and right, the Rheged men were tackling cavalry and chariots, and fighting hard. Dumnogenus was unhorsed, and disappeared beneath a wave of Picts. Dividing his men, Arthur launched flank attacks. The hated Picts stood their ground, and fought, but soon they, too, began to give way, to retreat, and finally, to flee.

Gaullac wiped sweat from his eyes; his horse's flanks, splashed with mud and gore, heaved as it stood, head lowered, exhausted. He said, 'It is finished.'

And Arthur looked down at the hacked corpse of Nudus, and smiled.

'Yes,' he said. 'It is finished.'

## Dead Space

*RJ Ashby*

I wake and in the gloom. I feel the space you left. You left it all to me, and yet your shadow loiters.
If I take your space — what of mine?
I filled your wardrobe full and now my clothes all hang, with room to breathe, as I conceal the chasm.
I organise my shoes. They stand together waiting for their time to come to take me out.
Your shoes could wait here too. I only have two feet and they can only wear two shoes.
The rest are just a show of choice — no use. They could all go in a box — too…
I organise my makeup. It stands so pretty, balancing up the space that always was mine.
How often does that space create the face you knew? Now my days to dance and play are gone.
You know you can come back.
You keep this space.
Your pillow waits each night for a head to rest, a cheek to flatten or a hair to tangle.
Your space is still — dead space.

## First Lesson

*Annis Farnell*

Far below, the great expanse of Lake Melville opened up, stretching west into blue distance. From her seat, Alice could see the little town for which they were heading. Odd, she thought, I never realised Rigolet was on an island. And which one of all these is Henrietta Island?

The nose dropped, and the light aircraft banked to line up for the final approach. Through the curtain separating the passengers from the flight deck, she could hear an incomprehensible chatter, the pilot's voice clear enough, but the rest drowned by static.

The town disappeared, and to her left now was an arm of the lake, bounded by tracts of brooding forest interspersed with viridian patches of bog, and streaked with outcrops of barren rock. The land stood in heavy ridges, ploughed by ice and carved by water, which threaded the deep valleys with runnels from trickles to torrents, and lapis lazuli lakes glinting in the sun. A harsh and unforgiving landscape, she thought, and a momentary wave of panic threatened to drown her. What on earth was she doing, coming to live in this godforsaken wilderness? Her eyes fell on the well-thumbed book in her lap. 'The Land God Gave to Cain'. Yup. That was it. Nothing like a bit of good, old-fashioned, romantic escapism, though perhaps extrapolating it into real life wasn't the brightest thing she had ever done. Ach well, too late to worry about it now. The wave receded, leaving her beached on a bank of excitement and optimism. The letter from the Newfoundland and Labrador Education Department had told her she would be met, and idly, she tried to imagine what the reception committee would be like. Some motherly creature, who would fuss over her, probably. She supposed she or he would have one of those hand-written placards, 'MISS ALICE GORDON' in shaky marker pen.

The plane swept past rooftops, and suddenly, there was tarmac, a bump and a rumble, and the craft was braking, braking, then turning to taxi sedately to the airfield building.

Looks more like Bert Elder's new byre than an airport terminal, Alice thought. Her parent's neighbour had been less than impressed with her plans.

'Teach in Canada? Are ye daft athegither, quine? Could ye nae jist fin' a schweel hereaboots?'

She chuckled at the memory, and so it was a smiling sprite of a woman that Rob McKenzie saw coming through the doors, the smile fading a little as she realised there was no placard bearing her name.

'How did you know who I was?' she asked naively, shaking hands with this hulk who had come to meet her.

Looks like an escapee from the cast of 'Grizzly Adams', she thought, taking in the long, grizzled plait and the gorse bush beard; all he needs is buckskins and a rifle in a fringed rawhide case. This updated version wore a red checked mackinaw over a green wool shirt, brown cords tucked into rigger boots, and, a concession to summer, a baseball cap. With difficulty, she retrieved her mangled fingers.

'Wasn't difficult, ma'am,' he replied. 'You were the only stranger on the plane. This your gear? Ain't got much, have you?'

'The heavy stuff got sent by sea,' she explained defensively. 'It should be here. Well, you know, at the docks. And I thought I could get anything I needed once I got here.'

'Well, there's Goose Bay, I guess,' he said doubtfully, shouldering her Army-surplus bergen. 'But it's a long ways. Sure, the teacher's house has some stuff, and I got you some groceries, but it's kinda basic.'

Oops. Oh, well, she'd manage. He ushered her into a taxi already loaded with grocery bags and a reel of barbed wire. Never mind the barbed wire, would the house have a freezer? she wondered. Of course it would; this was Canada, a civilised modern country. Wasn't it?

McKenzie whisked her into and out of the godown at the harbour, commandeering the services of a pair of Inuit en route to carry the heavy boxes of books down to a small fishing boat. He handed her down into the shelter of the wheelhouse, while the Inuit stowed the bags and boxes. The engine rumbled into life, and the boat's nose butted into the wavelets as she gathered way.

'There she is,' McKenzie said proudly. 'There's Henrietta'.

Henrietta, and a new-minted life. Alice breathed the scents of diesel and salt, fish and pine resin and none-too-distant ice, and knew she had come home.

## Force Eight Imminent: Rockall, Malin, Hebrides…

*RJ Ashby*

Clouds roll thick insulating and grey,
Menacing the wind bleached vista.
Pixels of rain angled curtains cussing my way.
They bully off-course by a push and a pull,
A spear and a blast, frenzying force.

The haul to the beach keeps me
buckled and bent,
sand-blasted and breathless,
hair matted – unkempt.
Sand storms – skitter,
smart in attack.
Leaving tear stained eye lines
From sand-blasted flack.

Avoiding the spume,
And the wet sinky sand.
Fly like a yacht running free,
Up the deep powdered strand.
Drowning in drifts,
Sand dunes resigned
Softly smoothed over,
Yesterday's redefined.

Tormented inland past the grey of the grass,
Prickled and prodded — as you pass.
Then —
Tack leeward —
And home.

## Herb Tea

*Annis Farnell*

Sit down, Susie, don't mind the cat, Grimalkin will shift for you, seeing you're family. Nice to know the younger generation is taking an interest, your mother couldn't wait to get away from us. Family myths? Don't talk to me about family myths, our lot have more stories than the Blue Fairy Book.

Would you like some tea? No, not that horrid black stuff, it's full of caffeine and carcinogens, I never touch it myself. Let me make you something nice and refreshing...let's see...lemon balm, with a hint of bergamot, and chamomile, yes, that'll do. Now, what was I saying? Oh, yes...

Take Great-Grandpa, for example: couldn't wait to get into khaki at the start of the First World War. Funnily enough, he never talked much about what happened after they gave him his kit; no heroic tales of derring-do and slaughter on the Western Front. Of course, it was classified as a Home Posting, so there weren't any of the benefits of being overseas, so maybe he just didn't think it was worth the effort. Either that, or the history books are telling something near the truth for once, and it was all just too horrible to think about.

Then he copped a Blighty at Wipers, that's Ypres to you and me, and while he was recovering, there was a call for volunteers for service overseas. Well, it couldn't be any worse than France, so he put his name down, and next thing anybody knew, they'd shipped him off to Palestine.

This is where he started telling about his adventures, and to hear him talk, he was best friends with Lawrence of Arabia. The family was awfully proud of that, until someone in the Seventies suggested Lawrence was gay. They played it down a lot after that.

Later, Great-Grandpa heard the magic word 'volunteer' again, and it took him to East Africa, where, naturally, he became indispensable to the success of Jan Smuts's campaign. Ah, well, we can all dream, can't we?

Then there was Uncle Desmond. Desmond had us all convinced as children that he was in the forefront of the Normandy Landings, and fought his way to Berlin with tremendous, if unsung, courage. Later, I found his birth certificate: 23rd July, 1931. As our American cousins would say, do the math.

Auntie Em — your Mum's named after her — she reinvented herself every time she dumped a husband, so we were never quite sure which guise she would present herself in next — débutante (he was Armenian, and thought she had Connections, as well as a British passport). Then she becomes an actress, resting, of course, until the ultimate grand part presented itself. Husband Number 2 never went to the theatre, but allowed himself to be dazzled. She became a model for Husband Mark III, an elderly type whose sole claim to fame was that he died before she got him into the Divorce Courts. You'll note that none of her personae worked in a solicitor's office typing interminable documents and making endless cups of tea, which is what she really did, until the alimony piled up enough for her not to bother.

I could go on, take you back in time to meet our romantically disreputable ancestors, but perhaps you've heard enough? One of ours was hanged, drawn and quartered for raising rents for his brother in exile. When? Oh, round about 1753; after the Jacobite Rising, anyway.

Who was my favourite? The witch, of course. She made quite a name for herself with her herbs and simples, and her...other talents.

It's a mistake, you know, to believe what they tell you in school, that they were all poor harmless old ladies with warts and no family; she could scry, and see auras, both of which I suspect came in very useful. That, of course, was where the herbs and simples came in: a love potion for a pair who didn't have the wit to see they were in love, a nice herbal tea with a spot of hemlock for a mother-in-law that clung onto life just that little bit too long, with maybe a dash of aconite if she'd been really nasty.

The herbs? Don't be silly, dear, of course I know about them. Your aura's gone a very funny colour, almost as if you were afraid. Do drink up your tea, you'll feel so much better after.

## How it Might Have Gone

*Elves*

We were both standing, each declining to take a seat. Seats were too permanent for what we were saying, too suggestive that we might linger.

'Laura,' I said, 'you're making a big mistake.'

'A mistake?' she snapped, in that way she did, in that way I loved. 'What sort of mistake?'

'You're misjudging me.'

'Oh yes?'

'And you'll regret it for the rest of your life.'

'The rest of my life?' I could almost feel her laughing at me. The words were like daggers, striking their blow against my unprotected ego. 'You do know how old I am, don't you?'

I was rattled, more than usually. Why was I being so cautious? Caution would lose the game. If I was ever going to be forthright, then this was the time.

'What's your point?' I said, hoping that she would catch the hint of aggression in my voice.

Her face showed no change. My arrow — Cupid's arrow — missed its mark.

'You seem to think that I'd want to stay with you forever,' she said, and her head jutted forward at me. Right in my face.

I reciprocated. 'That's right. That's exactly what I think.'

Her head jerked back. Had I caught her by surprise? Was that even possible?

'Charles,' she said, more softly than was her norm. 'That's unreasonable.'

In for a penny, in for a pound. 'Then tell me why you want to break up with me.'

'I don't want to break up with you.'

'Then why are you breaking up with me?'

'Because…'

'Because?'

'Well, I feel frustrated. You never argue or stand up for yourself.'

Gotcha, I thought, seeing a chink in the armour of her rationale.

'I'm certainly arguing with you now. I'm saying that you're being daft. I'm saying that you're going to hurt us both. And for no good reason at all.'

'You're the boy. You're supposed to take the lead.'

'That's really sexist,' I think I sneered as I spoke, as if at that moment I just didn't care. 'If it's true; which I doubt,' I added.

'It is true.'

Gotcha again. Her voice had taken on a sort of pleading note. I'll ease up.

'I want to share things with you,' I explained. 'I don't want to make every decision and just have you follow me whatever I say.'

'Even so, it's your job to take the lead.' Now she twisted her face away from me. She was having doubts, second thoughts. I would take advantage of her weakness.

'Is that how you want your life to turn out?'

'What's that supposed to mean?'

Wow, had I got that wrong? I swallowed, took a deep breath while my eyes didn't leave her.

'Always doing as you're told,' I said.

'Of course I don't.'

Phew. Position recovered. She was still trying to escape my eyes, looking anywhere but at me.

'But you want me to make all the decisions. And you'll follow me wherever I lead?'

'No I don't,' she pleaded. 'I just want you to take the lead some of the time.'

'Some of the time? And presumably you'll take the lead the rest of the time. So what do you suggest, a fifty-fifty split?'

'Don't be stupid. That would never work.'

'But neither does just saying that you want me to take the lead – but not all the time. You have to tell me what you want.'

'That's just the point. I want you to know what I want.'

'Laura! Please. That's just plain unreasonable. How can I know what you want if you don't tell me? We have to talk to each other.'

'So now I'm unreasonable?'

We stared at each other. This was on a knife-edge. Back from the brink maybe, but not certain yet. Let's give her a little push, like you might do when someone stands on a parapet and threatens to jump.

'Perhaps we're both being unreasonable,' I told her. 'Perhaps you're right. Perhaps we should break up.'

'But you think that if we talked more to each other …'

'About what we both want.'

'… then we could get on better?'

'I think so.'

Bingo.

'Ok. Let's give it a try,' she whispered. 'For another three months.'

I breathed a sigh of relief. I held the chair out for her and urged her to sit down. I took the other chair, but I didn't let her out of my sight for a moment.

'Are you going away for Christmas this year?' I asked, trying to sound normal, trying to hide my excitement.

'No. We're staying at home.'

'Let's go out as often as we can then. And sometimes just the two of us. Bill's having a party on the twenty-seventh.'

'I'm still not going to see you more than twice a week.'

My shoulders dropped. This wasn't going to be a new beginning then, just a temporary truce, a continuation of how it had been.

'Oh,' I said. 'Ok then.'

With no warning, her hands clenched into fists, her eyes narrowed to slits and she showed her teeth.

'Aargh!'

**I Love You, Son**

*Palo Stickland*

I'm 3
It's a party,
all the men laughing and drinking,
Dad likes his whisky and I watch the men.
They say, 'Go and play,' but
I stay safe, in the crook of my Dad's arm,
sitting on his knee
watching them.

My Dad was a strong man,
played hockey,
lifted engines by himself.
They said 'You'll be lucky to grow old,
don't work so hard.'
But he did.

I'm 13
He's tying a turban on my head
saying, 'This is who you are.
We're survivors.
Don't forget,
I love you, son.'

I'm 23
Driving through the night

to a strong man's passing.
'I'm here, Dad. Come on, breathe.'
Listening to his fading heartbeat
I hear the rhythm of my life.
'Don't forget
I love you, son.'

## In Sickness

*RJ Ashby*

At 15:36 Jessica stepped off the bus and took to the footpath, numb and confused. Her home was the same as it had been that morning. Carl too, would just be the same. Since that first date — wearing his cream linen jacket, shirt and tie — she had loved him.

'He doesn't look like he's from round here. Is there a posh part to Altrincham?' Her father asked when he picked her up.

'Opposites! Opposites attract Dad!' She pursed her lips to cover her grin. Twenty years later they were still married, and she still wondered how long it would last. In the last two hours things had changed. How could Carl love her — now?

Now…

Now the road took her home to Nightingale Drive. Jessica's pace had lost its skip and her eye had lost its focus.

The gate clicked open onto the usual order of their front garden: hedge shorn, grass cut and roses, red, yellow and pink, in bloom. She hesitated, three steps from the door... Then she turned, back to the road and walked away.

Home threatened!

Nightingale Drive was quiet. Each house the same, duplicated many times over; a garden, a drive, a garage and a polished front door with a burglar alarm set in the eaves. The street led her on as it curved leisurely towards the park, the lake and the sports ground.

Cancer? The doctor hadn't said cancer. A growth? The words tainted every thought and the sense in them exploded and she recoiled. Step by step she tried to remember.

The waiting room had been bland. The patients merged, colourless, faceless. She had felt out of place as she waited for her appointment, a smile drawn on her lips. She kept her coat buttoned tight. She was wasting their time. The signs – oncology – had brought the first falter to her step.

At 14:20 they called her. Mrs Jessica Roberts.

Twenty-five minutes and a scan later she returned to reception and looking neither right nor left, up nor down, she crossed the road to the bus stop.

She stood cheerless. Her face was set. Her eyes were vacant.

Just yesterday she had been fooling with Carl.

'Mum, just shut it!' A shout from upstairs started her giggling all over again.

'I could take on a nightshift at Asda,' she had offered. 'That would save money!'

'Or promotion?' Carl suggested. 'Headteacher. That would pay better.'

'I have trouble organising my class. Organising a school — I'd be a disaster! But I can dance.' She had pulled him to his feet. 'Come Dancing — we could enter…'

Her laughter had tinkled.

All from a blood test!

How did they know? Did I know?

I… I was fine.

Her hair was now sprinkled lightly with grey. The hairdresser was another routine in her timetabled life. He coloured and cut her hair, the same wavy bob that she had had forever. From when she had been single. Free to be herself. She had loved soft colours and ankle socks. She modelled herself on Sandy in Grease. She never quite progressed to the leather clad icon of the film, but then Carl was no Danny Zukko.

Every Saturday night she and Jane had gone dancing. Jane lived right next door then and they were like sisters. Jane with her crew cut and long legs: loud and minimalist. A photograph in the hall preserved their teenage 'joie de vivre': Jane's white knee length boots and hot pants. Pink round glasses defined her. She grinned over the top of them. Jessica's skirt flared wide in a swirl as she spun to look into the camera. Their grins were innocent.

No one noticed that photograph anymore.

'We'll send you another appointment… the consultant… City Hospital… And don't worry. We'll know better then.'

And don't worry…. Did they mean that? What if the appointment came and she couldn't go?

That would be a problem! A big problem! And another worry! How could she not worry?

She checked her watch. Carl would be finishing off at work now. He would have hung up his postbag, taken off his uniform. He would be heading for the football ground to coach the school team; Sian at centre forward.

Routines ran this family.

Wednesdays had always meant football. Carl trained with the local team. He really was too old, at fifty. Selection was by availability — and Carl was always available.

Carl's birthday – now that had been a worry. Everyone knew it was his birthday. Not everyone knew he was fifty.

'I'd love a surprise party. I'll pretend I didn't know.' He assured them.

Jennifer stood on guard, with a friend, and a ball, (for cover she insisted).

'He's coming. He's just turned the corner.' She shot into the kitchen and shouted into the garden. Voices hushed.

'Uncle Peter you can't come in here. Go out and hide!'

'I just wanted a beer.'

'Outside!' Jennifer's sounded like a practiced teacher.

The front door clicked.

'Anyone home?' His call was just a bit too bright. He was adorned for the part: tight black trousers, casual short sleeved shirt showing just the edge of a tattoo on his right bicep and a healthy, ageless, bald head gleaming with Jessica's tinted moisturiser on his weathered tan.

He called out again. 'Where is...?' His voice lifted in question. 'Jessica? Sian? Jen?' He turned to the garden and his eyes grew wider, and he gasped. 'Jessica... You naughty girl!'

And she fell in love with him all over again.

Jessica perched like a doll on the park bench.

Fifty. I'll never be there. The thought chilled her. It turned her to stone.

That was where this all started.

Insurance. Just a bloody insurance policy.

Advice about the best policies had been offered at Carl's work.

'The kids need protection – especially now. It's our job to protect and provide.' He was serious.

There'd be no policy now.

Alone, looking out over the lake, her world lost its colour. The water darkened as gusts of wind ruffled the surface and shadows loomed. The grey of her eyes fixed on the distant shore. Her heart beat. Tears brimmed.

Cancer – she knew it *was* cancer. There was something in the way the nurse had spoken. Something in the way she summoned the doctor. Jessica felt a truth.

Her mind strayed. A humble vision of a pupil played. Joe was now eleven. Cerebral palsy writhed through his limbs, his smile constant, a drool always on his chin. His electric wheelchair brought him a whisper of freedom. Jessica would take his hand and wait, watching and listening ready to decipher whatever came out — a twist, a smile, a grunt — sometimes all at once.

He had been in her class for two years. She hesitated in her fear for his future.

My future? She shifted her gaze.

When Jen had been a baby, tiny, only weeks old, Jessica had gone on a night out. Carl stayed home. But…

The smell of vomit had hit immediately. Carl peered from the top of the stairs. His face was grey. He was shaking.

'Mummy!'

Sian stood naked in the bathroom. There was vomit on the floor and in the sink. Garments flecked with sickness were scattered around. And Carl's shoes!

'Sick in her bed — hours ago. I just can't do sick Jess!' He had a hand over his nose and he retched.

Carl was supping a glass of whisky when Jessica made it back downstairs.

At 17:30 Jessica stood and lifted her bag onto her shoulder. The weight matched the pull on her heart and her steps home were slower and more considered. Her steps gave a rhythm. Cancer… And again, CANCER.

The word didn't freeze her brain any more.

She was ready.

A scream of excitement drove through the hall. The scream splintered her words and the excitement drowned them.

'Mum, Mum, I got in! I got in!' Sian's shout bounced off the walls and danced in circles and Jessica was thrown off centre.

'Oh My God!' Hands held, they stood staring at each other, Jessica absorbing the news.

'Look! Here, the letter!' Sian waved it. Jessica read carefully.

Staring at the letter, the blackness on white, swam, washed into insignificance. She blinked. And words formed.

'Oh Sian. I am so proud of you. Are you going to accept?'

Jessica turned, took her jacket off and moved to hang it in the hall cupboard. She rested, just for a moment, leaning into the shell of her family, inhaling the dry comfort of their coats, cushioned by tweed, wool and fleece, shrouded in gloom. The nest comforted.

And then Sian was at the front door, screaming, bouncing and dancing all over again. Carl and Jen absorbed this attack.

At bedtime Carl's quiet steps slipped by as she pretended to read.

'How did you get on today? It was your hospital appointment?'

Without a movement to her head or a catch in her voice, 'Nothing clear,' she said.

The silence of the night settled round Jessica. Chills followed sweats – and her head buzzed. The clock marked time. Every second stilled to be counted. When she thought Carl was asleep she crept to the kitchen. The kettle stuttered louder than ever as she cuddled into Carl's discarded fleece. It numbed her pain. The future dimmed. She concentrated on the dining table that carried the scars of family life. Each scar held a tale.

'Jessica?' Carl stood confused, his face creased from sleep.

'I have cancer.' She considered a blackened stain she had tried so often to polish out.

'What?' He gaped.

'Cancer. Carl, it is cancer. A tumour...' Her gaze challenged. She knew he didn't want to understand.

'What?' Concern coloured the word this time.

Her head drooped.

Carl, by habit, also clicked the kettle on. His face furrowed. He took in her words. The kettle beat. Seconds passed.

Then he turned and spoke. 'In sickness and in health girl... Football's gone. It's you and me now!'

'No more football?' She looked up. 'As easy as that?'

'That's it. Gone!'

'If I'd known I'd have done this...' Tears twisted into a smile.

'Wouldn't have worked.' He shook his head. 'I *am* fifty. Just need an excuse really.' He held out his hands to her. 'Your turn. Your game now. Come here, love.'

Their embrace waved in more tears.

'And I've always wanted to see Barcelona – playing anyone.'

**Inclusion:** the addition of something or somebody to, or the presence of somebody or something in, a group or mixture

*RJ Ashby*

The portly stature of the headmaster, Mr Robert Laidler, looms out over the crush hall as pupils file past. The sea of purple and black makes it easy for him to spot those without uniform or those interrupting the tidal rush of children. Knowing exactly who to shout at or who to challenge, is a skill, a skill he certainly had.

'Well, wee man...' the irony is lost on the spotty teenagers, or 'Hey, Scooby!' his finger catching the child and reeling it in to him. A childhood in Glasgow had taught him many things and he knows how to intimidate. He catches sight of his new Mercedes perched by the main door. He wonders if anyone will comment. Personal issues seldom come up in conversation these days. He misses his wife. She had known how to keep him in line.

He hears a phone ring out from his office. The meeting is about to start. He clears his throat and sets his smile. Sun shines through the blinds, striping across the carpet and out through the open door in his court: his decision if you are in — or out! The room is ordered, seats placed for two sides. For — the speech therapist, Lou Renton, then Dickie Burg, the Educational Psychologist, Dr Vernon, the paediatrician, Ms Smythe, the social worker and finally, Jo Waller, an occupational therapist who settle to wait. Conversation ripples between them, smiles of acknowledgement and nuggets of life are shared. They laugh, relax.

Mr Laidler, and two of his teaching staff, Miss Brown and Mrs Fuller, pause in conference outside the door. The two ladies are sent in to sit in opposition.

The family arrives: Mr and Mrs Banks, Amelie, reluctant, comes last. She is sat between her parents — Keith and Maggie — the mark of her syndrome on show: ruddy cheeks, slanting eyes and an uneasy caution. Beneath that is a teenager, small for her age, hair clipped in a bob, wearing a uniform of navy and gold.

The formality suits them all — except Keith. He knows the world of fresh air, hard work and the crudities of men. He shuffles, uncomfortable, exacerbated by the ironed shirt, the tie, the school seat and the airless room. Amelie reaches over and lays her podgy hand on his. He nods a smile. She pulls her serious face.

Mr Laidler, anchored by his oak desk, speaks first. 'We are just going to talk through the idea of Amelie becoming a pupil at this school. All of our pupils at the moment have an academic focus. I believe that is not why you want Amelie to come here.'

Reports, questions and opinions are given. Amelie sits. She takes a deep breath from time to time. She rests her head, awkward, on one hand, then the other, then on both... She crosses and uncrosses her legs in mimic of the doctor. Her eyes focus on the floor, on the desk, on her shoes and her feet try a tap, in time with Jo, whose foot is twitching. She watches her mother. Amelie reaches to pull a hair from her mother's mouth, and touches her hair into place. In turn her mother smiles and takes her hand… And forty minutes pass.

'Can we go, mum?' she whispers, bored with the formality of this exclusion. And everyone laughs.

'Amelie, what do you think? Would you like to come to this school?' The headmaster speaks. He considers her carefully as if he is not sure she will understand.

'Yes I would. My friend is here.'

'Who is your friend?' He looks surprised.

'Jennifer, Jennifer Jackson.'

'Yes I know Jennifer. She is in fifth year. You won't be in her class.' He almost laughs.

'I know that!' Her response is abrupt.

'Do you know anyone else?'

Amelie smiles a shy smile, drops her chin and peers across at Mrs Fuller. 'I know her, Mrs Fler.'

'Yes — I know you. I've been coming to your school to get to know you.' Mrs Fuller smiles gently, encouraging.

'I've got new shoes.' She lifts her feet for inspection, now she is included.

'Very nice. Just right for a high school girl.' Mrs Fuller smiles again.

Finally Keith speaks. He coughs, his speech is fast and he squirms like a naughty child. 'You better look after her. She's different. A child with Down's will always be different. She doesn't always understand. She's a great kid. She… she deserves respect. *You* will have to help her!' He points directly at the head teacher.

Mr Laidler diverts the challenge and points to his teachers, Mrs Fuller and Miss Brown.

So Amelie is to be a new pupil at Alston High School, in August.

Next morning, just before nine, a black taxi pulls up at the entrance to Kings Knowe Primary School. A bag falls out first and Amelie tumbles after it. It takes her a few seconds to stand tall balancing her bag on her right shoulder. Her coat has bunched up under the strap and she looks as if she might overbalance.

Voices call in welcome, 'Hi, Amelie.' 'Good morning Amelie.' She acknowledges each one with a smile or a story. One lady pulls Amelie's jacket straight and lifts her bag neatly into place, balanced again.

'Thanks, Simpson.'

'Good day yesterday?' Mrs Simpson, her support worker, is interested.

'I got a new book, Simpson.'

'What, from the high school?'

'Yep. In here.' The bag is off her shoulder again and she squats down. 'Look. Alston High School.' She waves it at Simpson.

'Oh that's great.' She hurries Amelie and her bag along the corridor and into a classroom.

Mrs Pringle is always prompt. 'Good morning, class. After the register I'll hear any news. Important ones will be typed for the news section in the corridor.' Mrs Pringle sits at her computer and she slips straight into the roll call.

Then Amelie's news is first. 'I got new shoes. I got a book 'bout Alston High School.'

Her teacher smiles, 'Josh, help Amelie get her news typed. The rest of you pair up and find out the rest of the news stories round the school. Be back ready to start writing at nine thirty-five.'

At break Amelie clusters with friends sharing crisps, shouting, laughing, jumping, while others hover: the drama of the playground. Amelie is included.

Late August and a breeze blows into the lethargy of summer. Browning lawns and fruiting trees signal the season's change, and in Amelie's bedroom a pile of carefully folded new clothes announce another change.

The breakfast table, readied, yet no one sits down. Keith, clock watching, hurries the kettle, the teapot, the toaster: everything needs shepherding today. And Maggie monitors the daughter. She hovers in the hall. Tiptoes to the bedroom door and listens. 'Have you got your shoes on yet?' Do you want some help to fasten them?'

'Mum!' Amelie groans.

Maggie smiles and goes in. 'Oh, well done. Can I brush your hair?'

'Is anyone coming for breakfast?' Keith calls, polite. 'Maggie, surely *you're* ready!'

'Just coming. Did you hear that, Amelie – he thinks I'm last!'

'Go, Mum.' Amelie follows.

'Where did you put your lunch money?'

'In my purse, silly!' Amelie shakes her head.

'And your purse?'

'My bag, look.' Amelie bends to unzip her new school bag – just the front pocket. 'See. Little Miss Nosey!' She pokes a finger at her Mum.

'Oh I just worry – no Simpson.' Maggie draws her hand through her hair again.

'What time is the taxi?' Keith is scanning the road. 'I can wait till he comes.'

'Eight thirty. I hope it's the same driver. Now, cereal, Amelie, and toast. Dad's got all that sorted.'

The taxi stops. He's been before.

'Oh it's Terry.' Terry lifts his finger and nods.

'Hi Terry. New school – remember.' Amelie is in charge.

'Wait one minute, my lady.' Keith has something very small in his hand. He bends over in front of Amelie and fixes a badge clearly on her school jumper. It is engraved. It says Amelie Banks, Alston Secondary School.

'Hey, Dad. It's great.' She tries to see it but her chin restricts her movement.

'Just in case you get tongue-tied. You can point to it.' He lets his hand touch her hair.

Then Keith and Maggie stand alone.

'She'll be fine Keith.' She lets his hand drop and gently punches his shoulder. 'Trust her. And don't you forget *your* lunch!'

The taxi crawls into the school grounds. The back door bursts open and Amelie grins.

'T's alright Terry. I know. See you.'

Terry hesitates. It's his first day too. He hovers, just far enough to see her safe.

The girl in the office peers at Amelie's badge.

'Hello, Amelie. I'm Ali. Can you wait here while I phone for Mrs Fuller?'

Amelie knows how to behave. No hugs. No kisses now. She waits silent — in line, a veneer of normality, doing just as she has been told.

Mrs Fuller sails into view and gently tacks through the queue, her head alert and nodding left and right in greeting until she drifts alongside Amelie.

'Good morning, Amelie. Remember me — Mrs Fuller?'

'Yes.' Her face set, no smile.

'Now, come with me. Registration. Down here. Room five.'

They tack away from the group and enter the current of children moving along the corridor to door number five. Mrs Fuller points to the large black digit that stands out just below the little window. She glances in, a habit, before reaching for the door handle and opening the empty classroom.

'You are the first in. Where do you want to sit?' Amelie moves to the desk nearest her and tries to sit, even though the seat is pushed under the desk. 'Pull the seat out. Take your bag off. That's better. Soon there are going to be twenty-five children in here. This is your class.'

'Sandra MacLean, she is too,' said Amelie.

Suddenly the door is thrown back and cracks into the cupboard.

'Hi, Miss, this is ma sista.' A small blonde uniformed girl is thrust through the door and left.

'Hi, you must be Jenny's sister. What's your name?'

'Marianne.' She peers like a dormouse.

'Come and sit with Amelie. You can look after each other today.' Marianne thrusts herself into the seat beside Amelie, more comfortable behind a desk. She smiles, shy with her new friend.

'I got a new bag and things.' Amelie unzips her bag and carefully lifts out a pencil case. 'Look.' She takes out one thing after another to show her friend, naming each item before carefully putting them back into the case. Marianne is impressed. She touches the cute rubber, the Justin Bieber ruler and the smart new pens.

The clamour of voices rise in the corridor and the gurgling flow of purple and black slows. A tumble of boys rolls into room five, knocking desks out of place. One is Billy Smart. He shouts. He trips over the bin. He falls into one seat then settles right at the back. Mrs Fuller frowns. Girls swagger in, scarves, hair and bags swinging, selecting seats together and quietening under the gaze of a teacher. Names are called and hands raised to punch the air or smack together. Sandra marches in with another girl from Kings Knowe. A buzz of excitement moderated by fear shines in different measures from each face: a reflection of maturity.

'Good morning, class. Looking and listening to me. Please.' Mr Smith commands with a nod and a smile. They take in the teacher — their teacher — Mr Smith, and he settles on his desk to talk. Amelie likes him. Billy jests. The teacher laughs back.

Day two, then three, then four, marks the same path to room five; the same assembly; the same registration; the same bell calls order for a new day. Amelie can be herself again: a cuddle for Mrs Fuller, a joke with the janitor and a new name for her auxiliary — Johnson. Her timetable is practised: her hesitant foundation firms. And all the same work that patterned her learning begins again: reading, writing, numbers — only now some is shared with her peers.

In technical they all make a wooden door hanger — to hang coats on.

'I can't do this!'

'Now Amelie, what is wrong? Tighten the vice. That's it… Now rub the wood with the sandpaper. OK? That is just perfect. Well done. I want all those edges rounded. Take your time.' He smiles.

In cooking they design a pizza topping.

'I'm not allowed tomato!'

'So what else can go on top of your pizza? Have a look at the ingredients at the front of the room. What do you like? Pineapple? Bacon?' Mrs Renwick listens.

'I like bacon.'

In music she sits behind a keyboard and wears headphones.

'I like this, Mrs Manderson.' Amelie's smile is wide, nodding in time to a beat.

'Let me hear you play then. Are you on number five already? Go.' She lifts her finger and beats time for the notes. Amelie copies the sequence exactly. 'Well done. Can you try number six now? It's your turn on the drums after Billy!' Mrs Manderson pats her on the shoulder.

In Art they all match colours and paint a sequence of squares before experimenting.

'Miss, there's black paint on the green one.' Amelie informs.

'Oh dear — can you clean it off? Do it at the sink.'

Amelie turns the tap on full and water sprays onto the paint and squishes all over her face and hair.

'Oh Miss…' Amelie screams.

'I didn't want you to have a shower, Amelie…' The class all laugh. Amelie stands tinged with green, and she hams it up (as only she can). Mrs Johnston collects a towel from the store to help. Billy brands her an alien. They all laugh again.

And on the surface everything is well – comments stutter round the armchairs in the staffroom.

The class in room five enjoys registration – voices rise and fall camouflaged in fun. Amelie is included.

On Wednesday, in English, Billy's work is held up for the class to see. Everyone laughs. He tears up his jotter, sets his jaw, and swears. Then Amelie fails. The girls huddle, one says, 'Go on – show us!' and Amelie does. She removes her jumper. She removes her blouse. She stands proud, a model in her white bra.

Giggles are muffled and silence snakes. The teacher stops typing.

'Shit! Amelie!' He is shouting now. 'What are you doing? Get that top back on.'

'I got a new…' Her voice wavers.

'Get that top back on! Someone help her, Sandra, Marianne.' Marianne carefully sorts her shirt and helps Amelie struggle into it. Amelie is trembling. Tears fall and her lip droops.

They have never seen Mr Smith shout. He paces, uneasy.

'Take Amelie to the office please.' He directs, pointing first to Amelie, then to the corridor. And like a convict Amelie has to wait outside the Headmaster's room and the story grows like a triffid in a hothouse — into scandal.

The staffroom sparks attitude. 'Can't be trusted.' 'Knew it would end badly…' 'Harlot,' 'Just immaturity, kids like her are always immature' 'She's too vulnerable… shouldn't be here,' 'What if Mr Smith had been alone?' 'Right guys — we will refuse to teach her,' 'The boys are at risk!' Then the Union steps in — and reason drops out.

Amelie is reassigned. Decisions are made while Amelie studies her stepping stones to literacy and numeracy. Her timetable is suspended. Art becomes a colouring task and music — the beat of a CD.

At two fifteen Maggie Banks parks her car in the school car park and trudges towards the entrance. Her steps are slow. The meeting has less of a welcome. Three people sit opposite her, the desk a division. Amelie goes home.

Then a letter details exclusion.

Sun again shines through the blinds and across the carpet in the Headmaster's office for the meeting. The staff lead from behind the desk. Support services advise from the right. Keith alone, uncomfortable, sits for his daughter.

'Do Amelie's classmates understand?' His question is simple. 'Why did they not stop her?' A look of confusion contorts his face. 'Are you sure she wasn't dared — or told?' He lifts his hands — a question.

'Absolutely not!'

'Amelie was wearing a new bra. She is a show off. It was totally in character — not at all suspicious. Do you know my daughter?' Keith's defence is earnest and his anger controlled. 'When you get something new do you not want to show it off to someone?'

Mr Laidler's Mercedes twinkles outside.

Keith speaks again. 'Amelie will be delighted to return on Monday. If there is another incident *I will be back* to formally ask for evidence of inclusion. I take it she still has a support worker at all times. I want her protected. Boys are a threat *to her*. Put that in your notes.' He points to the minutes. 'Get to know her yourself!'

Keith leaves.

'He has a point.' the psychologist says.

'Miss Brown — follow up on that.'

Miss Brown writes it down.

Even Billy promises to help. 'I'll keep her right sir.' He pursues her alliance. He jests. He jokes. He prods and pesters. And she loves it. She giggles. She holds his bag. She simpers by his side. 'Billy-no-mates' has a friend.

Mrs Johnston watches.

The school runs a disco where the boys move in packs while the girls hover, and in the darkness the flirting bodies smooch and some lips touch. Billy invites Amelie out into the darkness for a kiss…

At bedtime Amelie whispers to her mum, 'I've got a boyfriend.'

Maggie laughs, 'Oh yes, not Justin Bieber?'

'Billy-no-mates. He kissed me.'

'At the disco?' Maggie's tone sharpens.

'No silly, in the playground. We went in the dark.'

'That sounds a bit scary?'

'No mum he had my hand.'

'Just one kiss?'

Amelie giggles and pulls the covers up to her nose, 'No lots and lots.'

'And what else.' She keeps the even tone.

'And,' Amelie giggles again, 'It tickled.'

'What tickled, Amelie?' Maggie's face freezes.

'His hand.'

'Where did he tickle you, Amelie?'

'Oh all over.' She shivers.

'Did he touch your bottom?' Her voice is low and calm.

'Touched my pants, he liked my pants.'

'Did he just touch you with his hands?'

'Course, silly. His hands. And a kiss.'

'Kiss on your lips? Only on your lips?'

'Course, Mum. What's wrong?'

There is no sun this time, and the blinds are open in the headmaster's office. Mr Laidler sits opposite Keith, face to face, man to man. The headmaster listens. He apologises. His promises seem real, and they agree.

On Monday Mr Laidler is up early studying his drawer full of ties. His wife devoted a lifetime to collecting them — for fun; for events; for love; for work — each to soften the brittle 'weegie' she had married. He lifts out the brightest — a purple tie scattered with butterflies. It puts a lump in his throat! 'There, Mary. Surely no one can ignore this!'

After the first bell of the day Mr Laidler glances at his watch, lays his pen down. He walks from his office, halts for a second outside room five, checks his tie and goes in.

'Good morning, Mr Smith. Is everything alright in here?'

'Yes, sir!' The teacher says smartly. 'Nice tie, Sir!'

Mr Laidler smiles, 'What do *you* think of my tie, Amelie?' He fingers his tie.

Billy calls out. 'Nae flies on you, sir!'

Amelie nods. 'Nice, Sir. Not flies, Billy, flutter-bys.'

They all laugh.

## Mistress Goodwife

*Sue Cook*

Every year he asks me what I want for Christmas. Every year I tell him. Every year he gets what he thinks I really want. Books.

This year I asked for a tablet.

'A what?'

'A tablet. You know, like a small computer?' Everybody at work has them. They sit around the table at meetings and tap away constantly. Taking notes, looking up instant answers if someone raises a query that stumps the panel, Facebooking (is that even a word?). They book the next meeting on them. If the meetings get boring they play games. Me, I just sit there jotting notes on the back of the papers I printed out beforehand because I haven't got a tablet, have I?

'What do you want one of those for?'

I try explaining but he pushes his lips out, half pout, half pucker, and goes on about how expensive they are and how there are better options. And certainly I don't want an iPad do I. No, not one of those.

So I mention a new A-Z as well: I might as well get at least one book that I actually need because of the home visits I do for work and my old one has lost its cover and with it half the overview of the city. And it is five years out of date. Then I go off to buy paper and cards and scrub the house from top to bottom before putting up the decorations and buying the tree and the hundred-and-one other things a mum has to do before the Big Day.

When it comes his gift is easy to spot under the tree because of its bright yellow paper sealed with blue electrical tape and the corners that are the gift-wrapping equivalent of a bad hair day: not that he doesn't care, it's just that he doesn't understand. And it's a tablet-sized present and it has my name on it. At least it's the right size for a tablet *in a box*, I think, and my hopes are up and I very nearly rub my hands together as I reach for it. *Candy Crush here I come*. But no. As my fingers explore the sides of the parcel I realise it is too heavy for a tablet, and slightly flexible.

Books.

Plural.

Paperback. Not that I'm an expert or anything.

There are three of them. About keeping chickens. Where the hell did that come from?

I turn the pile upside down and over and round, separate them all out wondering if the

A-Z slipped in between maybe. But no, there is no A-Z.

'Ooh look, mummy, chick chicks.' My youngest falls on the books and starts pawing through the pages with chocolate-smeared fingers. She points to a skinny, black and white bird called a Sebright and adds, 'They're like the ones on the farm.'

'You mean the finca, darling,' he explains. 'In Spain they are called fincas.' And he goes on to proudly tell me how he was actually going to get me the whole shebang, a coop with chickens in ready for me to get going, have it in the garden all set up, with a ribbon on top and everything, except the woman at the chicken place said it's not the right time of year and maybe he'd do that for my birthday.

And I'm still wondering where the hell it all came from as I go to give the turkey one last baste.

So here we are, in June, the proud owners of three chickens and a lurid, plastic, all-in-one, fox-proof, water-proof, easy-clean, easy-move-it-about coop with built-on, green, wire run that cost about the same as the tablet I couldn't possibly need, perched under the horse chestnut tree for shade.

My youngest, and my eldest actually, are both pursuing the chickens around the run each with a handful of feed, which is necessary, apparently, to keep the birds in laying condition (there used to be a season for eggs, but not any more thanks to science) and for which it will take around a year's worth of eggs to recoup the cost. I watch as they carefully poke fingers through the chicken wire holding out one piece of grain at a time for the birds to take. As they are rescue birds they don't understand this hand-feeding and simply look puzzled and walk away only to be followed by squealing children who patiently try again.

The books say that battery hens have no concept of nest boxes and that even a cardboard box on its side will do at first and that they will probably drop their eggs everywhere to start with. One of them proves this statement to be correct by squatting and dropping as the kids whoop with delight.

'Look, mummy. Our first eggs. Can I keep it?'

My idea about keeping chickens is to have them scratching free in the back garden, pecking at the back door, being shooed out of the kitchen by a gingham-skirted, red-cheeked me. They would live off scraps and eat all the garden pests, keeping the slug population under control so that our vegetables would flourish with the minimum use of chemical coshes and no slipping out after dusk with torches and scissors, being bitten to death by late night insects when all I want to do is lay my head down and get an early night because I'm dog-tired and I've another early start in the morning. And that's all okay if your garden is chicken-proof or you live on a farm and you don't mind if the chickens get worms like the ones on the finca in Mallorca. But for a rectangular, Larchlap patch in Stockport you need a run and a regime to ensure health, happiness and hygiene. It's all there in the books.

And the problem with living off slugs is that slugs harbour a parasite that can grow into worms in the throat of young chickens and cause them to choke to death. I know my chickens aren't young but I don't want to watch any of my three rescue hens choking to death, not after we got them to give them a better life. None of my books mention this particular parasite: I have the internet to blame for that. Probably I should keep off the internet.

The chickens on the finca in Mallorca didn't have a coop. The adults flew up into the trees at night and roosted there. Until the chicks were able to fly, or otherwise scrabble into the low-branched line of conifers that marked the edge of square earth they called home, they remained on the ground snuggled under mother beneath a bush or in some other secluded spot. According to Jorge foxes were not a problem. Not like in Britain.

'They do not need to be in trees,' he told me, pointing to the chickens as they settled down to roost one evening. 'Is where they like to be. We go to bed. They go to tree.' But Jorge's chickens had worms. You could see them wriggling in the fresh, wet chicken squit they dropped everywhere.

He didn't have a problem with slugs though. Not with his dusty, hot, fertile earth.

I have a routine now. Every day I let them out in the morning and back in again at night, cleaning away the leftover greens at some point in between and sweeping up the squit (which goes on the compost heap) from the lurid baseboard which slides out from the lurid coop and dusting it lightly with wood shavings, another expense as neither of us is a carpenter, nor do we know anyone who is one. The feeders need a daily clean too, because what nobody tells you, not even the books, is that chickens crap everywhere, though I should have known this from the mess on the patio at the finca. Once a week the nest boxes have to be mucked out and given a dusting of flea powder and also I sit down and just watch the birds, see if they are behaving like hens or moping about as if they might be ill. I check their bottoms and weigh them up, not that I'm quite sure what I'm looking for yet. The books don't tell you to check for a cough or look for a gape, but thanks to the internet and the damp climate, and abundance of slugs I'm doing that all the time anyway: I haven't seen any signs yet. Twice a year I will need to take everything out of the coop and sterilise it. These times I have marked on my souvenir of Mallorca calendar in the kitchen. One wonders how the birds' ancestors ever survived in the wild.

I'm sure Granddad didn't do all this when he kept chickens at the bottom of the garden in the war. On the other hand, Grandma used to scrub the front step every week, make her own pastry and iron underwear, so maybe I'm wrong. Maybe I'm just assuming the birds were left to their own devices and the inside of that little wooden hut was in fact immaculate, a testament to a stout brush, Domestos and strong, sinewy arms that never saw the inside of gym. A social history blog I found mentions that runs were moved around regularly and that perch boards were cleaned daily. But it also says that the writer didn't know any wartime home that kept chickens that didn't have a man in it. So maybe Granddad did all that stuff and didn't mention it (why would he?) and Grandma just cooked with the eggs. What I don't know, will never know, is if Grandma ever had her own Jorge, an experienced POW perhaps, released during the day to help locals with husbandry.

'That was a great holiday, wasn't it? In Mallorca,' he says over a glass of wine one night after the kids are in bed and I'm reading a section on raising your own supply of chicks.

'Mmm.'

It's a complex affair, raising chicks. Don't let anyone tell you that you just let the hens get on with it. You need equipment, you need planning. Even in the war they had hot water bottles and fish tanks. And I'm wondering about a cockerel. What would the neighbours think? Or should we just buy in eggs. Or chicks. Somehow Jorge's chickens just got on with it. But it's warmer in Mallorca, and there were more chickens. He didn't seem to mind if one disappeared for a while, stopped eating.

'I remember you stalking the chickens along the line of pines, trying to sneak up on the baby ones, not realising they were all following behind you, thinking you were the farmer's wife bringing their feed ration.' He breaks off and laughs, a laugh I love to hear because it means he is relaxed and happy and I am happy when he is happy.

I smile and think about having chickens roosting in my horse chestnut because that is where they would like to be really, knowing it is impossible because in Mallorca, at the finca, there was nowhere else for the chickens to go but the land of Jorge and his parents. Here I'd be forever knocking on the doors of my neighbours or worrying about cats and dogs and foxes.

Jorge's finca was filled with dry earth and no slugs and his ancient mother fed them with corn every day. His chickens had room to wander but every reason to stay home because as far as the eye could see were olive trees clinging to a land bleached by hot sun. When the lean cats shook themselves even they gave off a cloud of fine dust.

'We should go back,' he says.

'Where? To Mallorca?'

'To the finca. You liked it there. I never saw you so happy. And in the evenings...' he jiggles his eyebrows because in the evenings I was still randy from the afternoons.

I smile. 'You should never go back,' I say. 'And anyway, remember what I was like when we went.'

'I remember. So stressed. Those migraines. I took the kids off every day, left you with some paracetamol and the chickens.'

And Jorge. Jorge didn't need to ask what I wanted. Jorge knew.

He continues: 'The kids loved it. Mucking about on the beach. No mummy telling them they'd had too many ice-creams. Worrying about how much sun cream they had on. Are you sure you don't want to go back?'

'To Mallorca, maybe. But it's never a good idea to go back to the place where you had the best holiday ever. You can only be disappointed next time.'

He sighs. 'Jorge was right.'

I look up from my book. He is staring at his glass of wine, a different sort of pout on his lips this time. 'Jorge? You've been talking to Jorge?'

His eyes flick to mine and his mouth lifts into a brief smile. 'He said I should ask. He said a husband should never book a holiday without first asking his wife, however good an idea he thought it was. I just thought you were so stressed again, before Christmas, it would cheer you up.'

There is logic in that, I suppose. I resume my perusal of the chapter on breeding, pictures of contented hens and fluffy chicks of various colours. 'Did he say anything else? Is he married yet?'

'Yes, and his wife is pregnant already.'

Another reason not to go back. I think briefly about the faceless wife, a raven-haired Spanish beauty perhaps, happily underneath a dusty, hot, fertile Jorge every siesta while I sit eating my lunch at my desk.

'And he said I should get you some chickens,' he adds.

Of course he did.

'You know how it goes, when he said they were fully booked for the weeks I wanted and I should ask you first anyway, we just got to chatting and I said I didn't know what to get you for Christmas. You were so stressed and you said you wanted the tablet for work and I knew you didn't really, you just thought you did but it was just to fit in with everybody else and you don't actually like the people you work with anyway. He said you needed chickens. You needed a connection with the earth, with the past, something to nurture that wasn't your family. Something about slow living. I didn't really understand that, to be honest.'

'You should send him a picture of the chickens,' I say. 'But not the coop.' I don't want him to think I've gone mad.

'Good idea.'

'Tell him they are happy. Tell him I am giving up my job.'

'Okay.'

There is a pause before he adds, 'What?' He looks at me slack-jawed, judging if I am joking or not, decides correctly that I am not. 'Where did that come from?'

From not having a new A-Z or a tablet. From not having the time to scrub my own doorstep or make our own pastry or iron underwear, not that I would do the last of those. Ever. Even Grandma stopped doing that at the end. And then there was what Jorge had said about farmers when we had been relaxing in each others' arms afterwards one afternoon and I'd asked him if his intended minded him sleeping with other women, the intended which in that highly rural, religious region he only ever got to meet in the presence of a chaperone.

He gave me his best philosophical smile. 'If you want a good farmer, you get man who knows to keep animals happy. If you want a good husband, you get one who knows to keep wife happy, no?'

I want to be a good wife.

I lean forward and hold his hand. 'We don't need the money,' I say, though all that chicken feed doesn't come cheap. Nor the wood shavings, the worming and flea powder, the apple-cider vinegar that appears essential to digestive health but I haven't quite worked out why yet, something about it being the chicken equivalent of probiotics. Then there's extra disinfectant, virucide.

I raise my eyebrows. 'I would be less stressed. Remember when I was less stressed?'

And if you don't, ask Jorge.

## Recipe for Paul

*Palo Stickland*

Paul, you ask me for a curry recipe. Why do I find that difficult? Let me explain how complicated these notions of 'recipe' and 'curry' are for me.

It is all tied up in my origins. My grandmother didn't read or write and my mother didn't link her literacy with her kitchen. At fourteen I left school and spent two years with her learning cooking and keeping house. She'd never followed a recipe and I don't like to do that either. This might be because being able to read had nothing to do with cooking in my past, but also, it could be, that I really can't do what I'm told.

I stopped cooking my handed-down-in-the-family version of 'Indian curry' when my Scottish stepchildren indicated a preference for shop-bought sauce on their food. Jars of Dolmio and Spanish Chicken took over from spices. The last straw was my fifteen-year-old stepson's refusal to come to the table when I'd cooked chicken legs (which he likes) in the traditional onion sauce — which I now know he hated. He was in a phase of eating only certain colours of food and brown was not tasty. Taking one look he said, 'I'm not eating that!' and disappeared into his room.

I asked him to come through and have something else, giving him the ultimatum that if he didn't come to the kitchen I would bring the food to his room and throw it over his bed. Which is what happened, but I stopped cooking onion-based sauce though the spices remained in my cupboard, and still do. I think it's from a need in my psyche to keep alive the memory of mud-coloured village kitchens with low fires fuelled by cow dung patties. In winter the portable coal fires (a version of barbecue) were used. And talking of those, my Glasgow-born son is new to the concept of open fires; following his attempts, (a meal of burnt food from his new, domed, free-standing barbecue) I advise him, next time, to invite his grandmother who might be the one to show him how it's done.

'Just don't be offended if she laughs at you,' I add. 'She'll say, why you want do this when you have big Aga oven? I was happy not to light fires when I come to Glasgow.'

Long years past, in my grandmother's kitchen, an area under a wooden staircase, where no one was allowed without washing their feet, I sat beside her watching her use her little wooden tray of spices, ground with a pestle and mortar.

Salt, turmeric (which has antiseptic qualities as well as colour), mircha (dried hot chilli peppers), garam masala made of seven ingredients including two kinds of cardamoms (green and large brown), peppercorns, cloves, cumin, cinnamon and bay leaves (all of which have heat-producing qualities — so use sparingly).

Are you bored yet, Paul? Curry powder did you say?

No, never curry powder. I try not to even touch the jar that contains the stuff. Throw it out, Paul.

And now to the food called 'curry'.

In the Punjab, 'curry' or 'khari' is made from left over (sour) yoghurt mixed with gram (chick-pea) flour. It is yellow in colour and has vegetable pakoras (it is a plural word — not pakora) left to soak in the mixture after it's cooked. A bit like spicy soup with croutons; you eat it with roti (chapatti). When the British first arrived in India it was to the Chennai and Kolkata areas (east and south-east) and I suspect a lot of Indian-origin vocabulary comes from there. It is a long way from the north-west, (two and a half days by train) so curry, as in vegetable curry, and chapatti too, are not words I knew as a child.

To cook north-western Indian curry (spicy yellow soup with pakora croutons) take a litre of yoghurt with a cup of gram flour, mix with a spoon or whisk and leave to settle for a couple of hours. And then if you have two 'fires' or hobs, which I expect you will, you could put the mix on to simmer while you fry the pakoras. Keep stirring the gram flour and yoghurt mix from time to time. If it becomes too thick add water. Oh, and we never taste from the pot as even chefs advocate we should. There is a scrupulousness in clean cooking. Take some out and place in a bowl to taste – never from the stirring spoon.

For the pakoras, take a cup of gram flour in a mixing bowl and add water to make a medium-thick paste (not too thin as it should coat the vegetables). Into this add one potato and one onion. If you have cauliflower with leaves, wash these, chop and add. You can add aubergine and spinach, if preferred. Depending on the amount of vegetables you may like to make up more of the gram flour mix which you can salt and spice to taste. Above spices are fine. Dried mango powder may be used to add a tang but you could use tomato ketchup.

You might be tempted to eat the pakoras before they ever get to the curry, they are very more-ish. If so, make lots, they won't be wasted. They'd be nice with a glass of wine, too, while you're cooking. Are you allowed wine if you have Parkinson's Paul? It doesn't seem to have affected your golf, at all. I hear you win most of the time.

Use a spoon to lift the vegetable mix and drop rounds into the heated oil. (Professional cooks use their fingers but I have been burnt by hot oil doing this.) Fry until cooked. Be careful to cook thoroughly as undercooked gram flour can upset your tummy. Lots of vegetables and less flour is best, not the round cheap, too floury balls from the supermarket (they are British not Punjabi Indian). And as for onion bhaji — I have never come across that in my home-cooking. Try not to let the liquid gram flour and vegetables mix lie too long, otherwise it sheds liquid and results in flat pakoras. Drain the pakoras on a paper towel and check your curry mix, which is simmering on the other hob. It should be of a smooth yellow, soupy texture and consistency.

Okay, the next step is the constant in Punjabi cooking. Fried onion sauce. This is used in almost all dishes. When I lived in the Punjab in the sixties, after the siesta, at about five o'clock the sound of sauce preparation (pestles on mortars) would come from every house, followed by the sizzling of the cooking oil and then the scootching sound of kneading dough and the clap of the tray against the floor. So, into your pestle (you could use your mixer with chopping attachment or liquidiser) place one chopped onion (medium size) and one inch of root ginger, chopped. Pound or mix. Now the spices. Freshly ground are the absolute best but time-consuming. Dry grind one large brown cardamom, half spoonful black peppercorns, cumin and poppy seeds, a half inch cinnamon stick, five cloves. During chopping or pounding add one teaspoon turmeric and salt (or to taste). Add the seeds of four green cardamom almost at the end of cooking with three bay leaves. If you only have ground garam masala, use it. You don't even have to grind or liquidise – heat some oil in a saucepan, add two chopped garlic cloves (if you have them and/or want to use them) and brown. Add chopped root ginger (if you don't have any then use one teaspoon ground ginger or miss out). Add chopped onions; fry till soft and light brown. Add salt, turmeric and spices. Add a half tin of chopped tomatoes. Cook until mixed, add water until well cooked. I never use flour in a sauce – my mother would be shocked.

In Indian restaurants the preparation for the onion sauce, which is in almost all the food, is the first act of the day. The onions are chopped by the kitchen staff at the end of the previous evening, left in a large pot of water, so that the cleaner can turn the gas on under them in the morning. They will cook for several hours under a low heat. I have a friend who has made a couple of million (pounds sterling) from providing 'curries' to customers in an affluent area of Glasgow. She was the cleaner before she took over the bar work and her duties included switching on the onions and cleaning out the toilets of the remains of too much alcohol. She wouldn't like me giving you this 'curry recipe'. She once told me not to tell people how I cooked Indian food. Her husband, in the days before the restaurants brought chefs over from India, took a book of mine to add to his repertoire of recipes. It is called 'Mrs Balbir Singh's Cookery'. It might still be in print. That reminds me, Paul, what you didn't say was, is this for personal or professional use? Are you diversifying from Italian to Indian? Only kidding.

Now the onion sauce is cooked, the next step is to pour in the gram flour 'soup'. Bring to the boil. Drop in the required number of pakoras, or as many as are left. They are very more-ish, aren't they? They will swell, so not too many. Bring to the boil. Take off the heat and you have Punjabi Curry. Serve with roti or other bread. If you ate all the pakoras, you could chop potatoes, boil and throw them in to the curry.

Punjabi Curry is a really cheap, leftovers kind of dish. To make any more expensive meat or vegetables dish you use the same sauce. Fewer onions, less spices, no tomatoes or more, add yoghurt or nuts. It's all variations.

Now, over to you! Happy cooking Paul, and do lots! I think that really is the secret.

## Silent Messages

*Mairibeth MacMillan*

There was something in the air today — maybe it was autumn. Even with my hands thrust deep in my jacket pockets, I could barely feel my fingers as I sauntered up the hill towards the school. A woman pushing a buggy rushed up behind me, careening onto the road to pass me. Why was she in such a hurry? There were ten more minutes until the bell. She didn't even say hello.

Despite being early, there were already lots of parents waiting in the playground. The usual laughter and chatter seemed muted. Everyone seemed to be watching the school doors. I nodded to a dad who caught my eye then just turned away. I smiled at a mum I knew from Toddlers but she just stared back. I walked up to where three of my friends were standing, huddled together. I heard the word 'vicious' and 'attack' and 'ambulance' and could feel my heart start to pound. I opened my mouth to ask them what was going on but they took a step away from me then another and another. Not one of them would look at me.

I looked around, noticed a police car pull into the staff car park. When I turned back around one woman stared right at me then shook her head and turned away. What had happened? I swallowed, had to try more than once because my throat was dry and there seemed to be a lump in it. Had something happened to my son? To my little boy and none of them could bring themselves to tell me?

Fighting back tears, I took a step towards the school door then another and another. I clenched my fists in an attempt to stop the tremors and the creeping coldness that were moving through me. Two policemen headed for the school door where the Head waited. When she noticed me her lips pursed.

'Mrs Miller,' she said in a toneless voice. 'We've been trying to contact you.' I stopped breathing. My phone was on silent. I'd been in the garden. I hadn't checked it in hours. 'There's been an incident.'

'Is Michael all right?' I pushed past her but stopped when I saw my son sitting on a chair outside her office. He looked up at me his eyes angry and then I knew. Whatever had happened — my son wasn't the victim.

## Speaking Nonsense

*Enza Vynn-Cara*

I'm no good with words
or praise.
I say what I feel
yet think otherwise.
And still am honest — perhaps.

But now I think I should
say more,
speak nonsense,
tell you

your smile
stops
arrows in flight
sieves
gold from copper,
truth from lies,
comfort from stagnant idleness.

Your voice transmutes
water to wine,
serenity to happiness,
calm to glory, tomorrow more than yesterday.

I should tell you

all this
before winter's glow tinges
violet-blue the shadow of the night.

Yet, I fade back
into my worn-out self,
a shy unsung spirit,
wanting to be alone and not lose you.

To think I love you is easy,
to say I do
is speaking nonsense.

## Tainted Tube Love

*R. Cohen*

I love the rat-a-tat of your wheels on the track,
the jig and judder as you worm down in the black.
The camaraderie of me and the others all stuck,
in the tunnels as your signals fail, we curse our luck.
We roll our eyes in unison and as one we loudly tut,
trapped on the Central Line, another power cut.

Shoulder to shoulder, crammed in as we wait,
your carriage becomes a dressing room under Lancaster Gate.
Wielding a mascara wand a woman starts to preen,
she's still adding makeup as we're held at Bethnal Green.
Her boring office dress is shed, so too the practical flat shoes,
and she's ready to hit Chigwell in a pair of Jimmy Choos.

We love to moan and mutter at your service and delays,

the overcrowding and extreme heat or general passenger malaise.
But without you we'd be worse off, the day an utter mess,
crossing London on the buses? What a nightmare, what a stress!
As commuters we're all horrid, and most of us are rude,
but don't take our grumbles seriously; we love you, dear old Tube.

## The Baby

*Palo Stickland*

Nina finished loading the dishwasher, sighed, wondering when this had become her job, when she heard Tony's feet on the stairs.

'Nina, Nina. There's a … a bat!' He burst through the door, arms spread, fingers gesturing for help.

'You knew there were bats here, when we moved into the area. They're a protected species, don't harm it.'

'Nina! It's in our bedroom. We must call Rentokil.'

'You're overreacting. It's much smaller than you.'

'It might be rabid! It's bound to be carrying fleas.'

'No, it's probably desperate to get out. Can't you open the window?' She turned to switch the dishwasher on.

'I tried, Nina. Really I did, don't look at me like that. I haven't lived in the country before. It swooped at my head.'

'No, it wouldn't have. I'll look.' She hung up the dishtowel, sighing again. 'You only had to help it to leave.'

Nina climbed the steep, wooden stairs of their cottage, with Tony creeping up behind her. As she entered their bedroom, he pushed her in, slammed the door shut, and fixed a chair under the handle on the outside.

'Tony, let me out. Stop being silly.' Too late, she heard the clatter of his feet going down.

Scanning the room for the bat, she spotted it perched on the wall light over their bed. A tiny bundle of black fur, pointed ears sticking up on the background of white paint. It swooped to the top of the wardrobe and back again.

'Tony,' Nina shouted through the keyhole, 'it's only a baby.'

Bending her head, at the same time as keeping an eye on the bat's movements, she slid to the floor, edging her way to the window, opening it wide, giving the bat a chance to find its way home. She kept low and waited. After a while the bat made a final sideways swoop to the top of the wardrobe on the opposite wall then swung right out into the darkening twilight. She watched it disappear into the trees at the bottom of the garden, marvelling at the agility of the tiny creature.

*Must've heard your mother calling,* she thought. *I wish it were as easy for me as it's been for her to produce an offspring.* Time and Nina's career had come first but now she was ready, it couldn't be with just anyone. She'd hoped Tony was Mr Right. Recently, she'd been wondering and now … she turned to call him, to give him one more chance.

No answer. He'd trapped her in the room because of his own fear. She stood in the window, looking towards the shimmering lights of the neighbouring farmhouse, making her decision. Then she acted.

Two hours later, the door of the bedroom was opened by a man wearing a Rentokil logo on his jacket, Tony peering over his shoulder. Nina walked past them, suitcase in hand.

'Goodbye Tony. The baby's gone.'

## The Calling

*Enza Vynn-Cara*

I dreamed I was dead
as dead as you and He
I asked how it is
you answered 'Come with me.'

'It's deep, it's dark
and we don't get to keep our hearts.
Down there, the eternal fire warms us cold, you see.'

I said that it couldn't be
I was good, sin-free
a faithful Christian through and through.

'How so',
you said,
'what does it mean?
You kept your trousers on and your nose clean?'

'That and more.'

Deep in the bottomless pit,
I couldn't see
beyond you, beyond He.

'How far?' I asked.
'Surely this isn't for me.
I rose to the pulpit and spoke the creed.'

'Where so?
within the walls of the chapel,
the safe haven of your bed?'

I said I followed
the teaching of our Father,
'The Bible is still in my hand, see?'

'Indeed,' you said,
'the psalms you fed
to each and all with a yawn.
You prayed,
turned the other cheek,
shut your eyes, put wax
in your ears — no sounds to fear.

Amateur, you missed the call!'

## The Death of Adonis

*R. Cohen*

Once a golden god, an idolatrist's dream.
Worshipped. Adored in boundless awe.
All eyes upon him, devoured by lustful gazes,
but the hunger fades into disbelief.

His blond hair of youth turned to grey.
A cheeky wink now wrinkled.
Body marching south as if to Rhodes
not travelled, a lifetime's journey interrupted.

What is beauty but a distorted mirror?
Young or old: a reflection of the unreal.
Never more than a passing image,
the wonders of last week's news cast aside.

The crone smiles at him, a knowing smirk.
Offers eye of newt to smooth crow's feet.
Toxin-laden lotion to unfurl a worried brow
or tincture of boar's tusk to peel away the years.

When the potions fail to work, cut out the old.
Flying knives, sharp as ravens' beaks.
Changes no longer just skin-deep emerge
reveals Narcissus, who revels at centre stage.

## The Goldcrest

*Annis Farnell*

I left the workshop door
    open, and in he came,
youth invincible, eager,
    flame-bright with explorer's zeal.
What brought him in? What drew him?
I came back, and heard
    the quiet, inquiring cheep.
He couldn't stay in my world,
    and so I tried to oust him,
Kind, not cruel.
Back and forth, and round
    he went, flirting with
the air, while I,
    clumsy, earth-bound, lumbered
stumbling in pursuit.
Tired at last, he flittered down
    behind the potting shelves.
I reached in, felt the anxious flutter,
    grasped and withdrew him,
weightless in my hand.
But freedom lay beyond him still:
    cobwebs twined his feet
shackling him. I tugged them free,
    fearful as he was, needle-thin
fragile legs, so easy to break.

At last, an aching æon on,
    the sticky bonds came free,
leaving limbs stiff, unmoving, useless.
    And so we sat a while,
and watched each other.
I saw, within the shelter of my hand,
    the long, thin beak, large,
liquid, brilliant fearless eyes,
    and bright across his head
a crown of fiery gold.
Then little claws came back to life
    and grasped my finger
with a newborn's clutch.
    I lifted away the shielding hand.
He leaped skywards, and was gone.

## The Green Room

*Sue Cook*

'If you leave a room unused for too long it gets haunted.' That's what my Gran used to say. Even as a child I thought this was dubious, the sort of thing grown-ups tell you to make you behave or to make life more interesting than it really is. It's definitely more exciting than the truth, which was that Gran sometimes slept in Uncle Jeremy's old room because Granddad snored.

But now that I have an empty room of my own I sometimes wonder if there was some truth in it after all.

The green bedroom was suspicious before we even moved in. It was tucked away in a Victorian extension that somehow still had not integrated into the mostly Georgian house. It was as if someone had stuck a cornflake packet on the side of a doll's house and cut a solitary doorway through the dividing wall.

There were two peculiar things about the room itself. First was its size. Most of the rooms in the extension were small, in keeping with the servants' quarters that we were told they once were, but the Green Room was a generous double bedroom.

The second oddity was the old built-in cupboards.

'Georgian,' said the surveyor who checked the house for the mortgage. 'Original.'

'How can they be older than the room?' I asked.

'Probably they were taken from another room in the house.'

'But there aren't any old cupboards in the rest of the house.'

'No, they're in there,' he said, with ineffable logic.

Why would the owner take out some old cupboards he presumably had no more use for and then refit them to a brand new room? It didn't make sense. I preferred to think of them as magical cupboards, cupboards that had floated invisibly in mid air until the room was built around them. Cupboards like that were capable of anything: they were Narnia cupboards.

The house had two spare bedrooms, both named after their colour schemes — the Green Room, of course, and the Terracotta Room. House guests always chose the latter so eventually we stopped even making the Green one up.

'It's tucked away at the back of the house,' Steve answered with a shrug when I asked why he thought no one ever slept there. 'Dark. Overhung by the trees from the garden. And that wallpaper is so…so…green.'

'But it's got all that lovely old furniture.' We'd bought it as a job lot from the vendors as they didn't want it. They'd also bought it from the previous vendors and had a feeling that the owners before them had done the same. It was as though no one wanted it. And I suppose you could see why. The bed was a magnificent Victorian thing, as old as the extension. But the mattress rested on what looked like a huge sheet of heavy-duty chain mail that was slung between the metal frame. The head and foot of it were polished hardwood.

'That bed, though,' Steve said on cue. 'That spring thing rolls you into the middle. And the carvings on the headboard,' he paused and did an exaggerated shiver.

'What's wrong with them?'

'The expressions on the faces are different every time you look at them.'

'Oh?' I was surprised. I didn't know he ever went in there.

'You can't help it, though, can you?' he said, as though reading my thoughts. 'There's something that draws you to the door when you pass it on the way to the bog.'

He was right. There was a magnetism about the room, something that lured you in. But I hadn't noticed the faces. I thought the carvings on the headboard were inanimate scrolls and flowers.

After our first baby was born I gave up work and stayed home with him. He was not an easy child, frequently screaming for endless hours during the day and night until I thought my head might explode with noise and fatigue. My mother said I had been just the same and it was a phase that would pass. The doctor said it was wind and it was a phase that would pass. What I discovered was, if I left him in his basket in the Green Room, he would instantly quiet.

The relief was so great that I didn't stop to question it. I just left him in there and put my head down to catch up on some sleep. Sometimes when I went to check on him I thought from the corner of my eye I saw the basket gently moving. But as soon as I looked directly at it, it was as still as the house and the baby was at peace.

One day I saw a picture of our house on the front of a local history magazine, so I bought it.

It was there to illustrate an article about our village. I read through and learned that our home had at various times been a pub, a doctor's house and a manor house for one of many small parishes hereabouts.

What I couldn't find was anything that might explain the mysteries of the Green Room.

I emailed the editor. He passed my query to a member of the local history group who he thought might be able to help. Meanwhile the baby slept quietly in there and I'd renamed it Joe's room, after him.

The man who knew about our house was called Gerald and spent three months of the year in Spain. He promised that when he returned he would bring photographs of the house and talk to me about it. He added, 'This is the problem with you incomers. You push out the local knowledge.'

I didn't know what to make of that. We all have to live somewhere and I'd been brought up in a city where we were all incomers. Our estate had been so new that probably there was no local history; nothing that went beyond a generation or so would be lost by my leaving. And probably Gerald was just as much an incomer in Spain.

By the time Gerald visited, Joe was sleeping on his own at night in his room. His cot was against the far wall beyond the bed. The Georgian cupboards provided ample space for all his clothes and paraphernalia and somehow seemed to need little effort to stay tidy. I slung things in any old how it seemed, but next time I looked everything was in neat piles. Maybe I was thinking more about Joe than the task in hand. Certainly I always felt a deep sense of calm in there, so probably I arranged things in orderly fashion without thinking about it. Joe slept all night long and so did I. In fact I was able to leave him in his play pen for hours on end and get on with my life like I had before. I even contacted my boss and asked if I could start doing some work at home, as most of what I did involved writing and proofreading. Plans were well advanced and I was looking forward to having a purpose in life again, beyond housework.

Gerald wasn't as old as I'd imagined. I had in my mind a village elder, bent as a hilltop hawthorn, white as a shroud, skin as marked as a battlefield. The reality was a tall, erect man with a shaved head, a healthy tan and small, lively eyes that missed nothing.

He insisted on seeing the bedroom at the back of house first. I knew exactly which one he meant and led him up the stairs to where Joe was sitting in his playpen apparently looking and burbling at something between him and the bed. Gerald's mouth tightened.

'I'd get him out of there,' he said. He refused to go back down to the kitchen and the coffee and home made cakes I had waiting until I picked Joe up and carried him with us. Joe whined and squirmed, stretching himself towards his pen.

Gerald's jaw muscles remained tight and he shook his head.

In the kitchen he pulled out a folder of black and white photos, many faded with age. As we looked through them he asked me if I noticed anything in particular. I didn't at first then he asked me to concentrate on the ones taken from behind the house. It took a while to realise that in every photo the same face, pale and ethereal, sometimes to the point of hardly being there, was present at the window of Joe's room.

He nodded once as I said this. 'What age do you think she is?'

I checked the photos again. 'Mid-twenties?' I guessed. And Victorian, probably. She had on a dark dress fastened to the neck. Her hair was pulled back and austere. The only visible flesh was her pallid face.

'Now check the age of the photos,' he said.

I did and as Joe's cries grew louder, my heart pumped faster.

'These span fifty years and she's always there. Always the same,' I said. 'Never looks any older. Who is she?'

'The doctor who lived here had a daughter named Emily. It's rumoured she got pregnant, though nobody knows who by and she was never seen again after. An extension to the house was built at about that time and it is said that room was her prison. The servants were not locals and no one ever really knew quite what went on there.'

'What happened to the baby?' I asked, still gazing at one photo after another.

He shrugged. 'Another mystery. Some say it died at birth. Some that it was taken away and given to a relative.'

I looked at Joe who was screaming like a thing possessed. 'That's why Joe likes it in there? She…Emily…is looking after him?'

Again he shrugged. 'That's not for me to say. What I can tell you is that no child brought up in that room ever lived to see its first birthday.'

For the rest of the day I kept Joe with me, determined he would not go in the Green Room again. But he screamed almost constantly and by evening the door beckoned.

I told Steve about Gerald's visit, showed him the photos that he had left and recounted the story of Emily.

'We've got a real live ghost,' he said, his eyes flitting between the same face on images taken fifty years apart. 'You hear that, Joe?' He turned to tickle our son's cheek. 'You've got a ghost for a nanny.' Joe, for a change, responded with a chuckle and a huge grin.

I didn't tell Steve the rest of the story. I was frazzled and I needed to sleep. I let him settle Joe down in his cot in his room and told myself it was just for a few more nights. After all, it was just a phase he was going through. It would pass.

## The Milkman's Apprentice

*Julia Chalkley*

Teddy woke at his mother's touch on his shoulder.

'Teddy,' she said softly. 'Time to get up.'

Outside his window, the sky was lit as he had seen it on clear winter mornings. The blue of the highest part of the sky was a royal colour, an imperial colour, and made him wish briefly that he was going to school later, with the chance of using their paints and coloured pencils in the lunch break to catch the scene on paper. When he sat up in bed, he saw the stripe of bright gold above the horizon that warned of the sun's rise.

He crawled out of bed and pulled on his clothes quickly before the chilly air dispersed the warmth from his skin. He went quietly into the front room, where the fire boomed and glowed in the fireplace, and his mother waited with a cup of milk and a slice of bread and dripping.

He ate quickly, knowing that he had only fifteen minutes before he had to be at work. If he was late, Mr Chivers would clip his ears for him and send him home. There were enough lads keen to take the job that he could be replaced within hours. This was a good job, too, one he could still do when he went back to school. If his parents wanted him to go back to school this year.

As he went to the front door, his mother said quietly, 'Happy birthday, Teddy.'

'Thanks Mum,' he said, looking back to smile as he shut the door. Thirteen, he thought. I'm thirteen now. And I'm the one earning the money, not Dad. I'm the man of the house.

It was even colder outside. The breeze was light, but it whipped at his jacket and blew cold air up against his shirt and around his face and ears. He kept his hands jammed into his pockets as he trotted the short distance to Chivers' Dairy.

As he turned the corner, he saw that the lights were on in the dairy. He made his way to the side door he'd been shown the week before, and let himself in. Inside, the shed was warm and alive with cows, huge creatures with the same long eyelashes and bulbous brown eyes as Betty Boop.

Mr Chivers was already at work, sitting on an upturned wooden crate, milking one of the cows. A row of buckets stood along the side of the shed, full of milk.

'Nearly finished,' he said. 'Pour them buckets into the cask in the middle there.'

Teddy took a bucket over to the big wooden cask in the centre of the yard and hoisted it unsteadily to shoulder height, He tipped it up and sloshed milk in big splattery batches into the cask.

'Quicker,' Mr Chivers said. Teddy put down his emptied bucket with a crash, and ran to get another. As he was pouring his fourth bucket, Mr Chivers came to stand on the opposite side of the cask and poured water into the warm foamy mass of milk.

Teddy faltered, setting his half-emptied bucket on the side of the cask as he watched. Water. It was definitely water. Mr Chivers was watering down the milk.

'Don't stop,' Mr Chivers ordered, glaring straight at him. Teddy thought of his mother, slicing bread so thin it tore, and scraping lard carefully onto each slice except for her own, and nodded, dropping his eyes to the task of pouring milk into the cask.

Mr Chivers kept pouring water, one bucket of water for each bucket of milk that Teddy poured. His final task was to take a long wooden pole from the door, wipe it roughly along its entire length with a rag and plunge it into the cask, stirring it strongly until the edge of the circling milk rose close to the lip of the cask, and the whirling centre of the liquid was a white pit like creased silk. He picked a length of dirty straw from the wrinkled surface without breaking the rhythm of the stir and flicked it away over his shoulder.

By the time they had finished filling and capping bottles with the watery mixture, Teddy was cold and wet and beginning to wish he could return to his bed. He felt sore along his shoulders and his eyes were hot and dry, ready to close and let him sleep in the mucky straw under his feet.

'Put 'em in crates and get 'em on the wagon,' Mr Chivers said. He was slotting the full bottles into wooden crates, picking up four bottles at a time and letting them drop into their places in a steady thumping rattle like a machine gun fire. He grabbed the handles of the full crate and hefted it onto the back of the wagon waiting at the back of the shed, turning immediately to the next empty crate.

Teddy began to load crates, the warm glass slipping between his wet fingers. He dropped one bottle, and it smashed on the concrete floor.

'Careful!'

'Sorry Mr Chivers,' Teddy said. 'It was an accident, honest it was.'

'That one comes out'a your wages,' Mr Chivers said.

Teddy slowed after that, loading more carefully. The milk in the bottles was cooling now, but he felt hot in his thin jacket and longed to take it off. He struggled to get the full crates high enough to get them onto the bed of the wagon.

'Finish off,' Mr Chivers said, 'I'll get Alfie, an' we'll get going.'

After Mr Chivers turned away to the stables, Teddy fetched an empty crate and turned it upside down to use it as a step. After that, he got into the rhythm of picking up a full crate, hopping up onto the step, stowing the crate onto the wagon and jumping down. It was like being in PE at school.

By the time Mr Chivers had hitched the horse into the shafts and opened the doors to the street, Teddy was sweating. Outside, the sun was fully up and the day was bright but still cool. The church clock clunked up to twenty to seven as he looked up at it.

Teddy's job was to carry the milk to the doorsteps. It sounded easy until he realised that Mr Chivers wasn't going to stop at each house. Instead, the horse went on at a slow walk, with Teddy reaching up into the crates, grabbing two pints and running to the doorstep to deposit them and to pick up the empties, while Mr Chivers kept up a steady monologue of customers' orders.

'Number fifty-three, two bottles. Number fifty-four, one pint. Number fifty-five, one pint. Number fifty-six, three pints…'

Some of the empty bottles on the doorsteps were still streaked with stinking milk. His mum always insisted on washing hers before putting them out for collection, and Teddy thought he'd tell her tonight that he appreciated it.

As they turned into Gladstone Road, Mr Chivers turned back to look into the crates in the back of the wagon.

'Still some left.' He looked at Teddy. 'Can I trust you?'

Teddy nodded.

'Right. Hop up here,' and he patted the driver's seat. Teddy scrambled up onto the seat. 'Hold the reins.'

As Teddy took the reins, Alfie snorted and began to trot a little faster. Mr Chivers said 'Hyup, hold!' to Alfie, and 'Hold the reins back, let 'im know you're here,' to Teddy.

Teddy pulled gingerly back on the reins, and Alfie slowed, stamping his huge hooves on the road.

'Let 'im walk on,' Mr Chivers said. 'If 'e tries to run off, pull 'ard back on the reins and holler 'Hold!' to 'im. Get down the bottom 'ere, turn left an' you're at the yard. Alfie knows 'is way home. Call out 'Milk!' as you go, an' if anyone wants a pint they'll stop you.'

Mr Chivers slid down off the seat and gave Alfie a hard slap on his enormous rough-haired rump. Alfie moved off at a slow walk, with Teddy clinging onto the reins. He needed to pee, really badly, but he didn't know where he could go, or what he could do with Alfie if he got off the wagon. He turned on the seat to call back to Mr Chivers.

Mr Chivers was standing at the door of the third house from the end of Gladstone Road. As Teddy got up his courage to shout for help, he saw the door opened by a woman in a smeared pinafore, with hair that looked somehow ragged and knotted at the same time. Mr Chivers took one long step across the threshold and the door closed behind them both.

Teddy turned back. Alfie was walking slowly down the centre of the road. If another cart appeared now, Teddy was relying on them to get out of Alfie's way, because he had never steered a horse before. He tried pulling on the reins, gently at first and then hauling at them with all of his weight and strength. Alfie took no notice at all, clopping steadily down Gladstone Road to the end, turning left into Margaret Street and finally stopping at the immense gates of Chivers' Dairy.

After a minute, Teddy dared to slide down from the seat, trusting that Alfie wouldn't move while he got the latch lifted. As soon as the doors started to open, Alfie moved forward while Teddy struggled to get the doors open enough to let the wagon in behind the horse.

Teddy ran to the netty and pissed for a long time, jiggling and whimpering with relief as he did. He could hear a steady rhythmic thudding in the yard. When he'd finished pulling the chain and buttoning his flies, he returned to the yard. He saw that Alfie had somehow unlatched his stable door and gone in. He still had the wagon full of crates hitched to his harness, and it was too big to fit into the stable – as Alfie strained to get at the hay in his manger, he was pulling the wagon against the outer stable walls, making them shake. The cows were bellowing in the yard.

When Mr Chivers returned, Teddy was still struggling with the harness straps and buckles, trying to release Alfie and keep away from those deadly hooves.

'Useless,' he said, opening the buckles with a few twists and tugs. 'Never 'andled an 'orse before, 'ave yer?'

'No sir,' Teddy said quietly.

'Bah.'

Within a few minutes, the wagon was unhitched and rolled away into its place. Teddy did whatever he was told — unloading the crates, putting the full ones into the cool room, washing the empty bottles in bleach and hot water, scrubbing the cask and buckets. Mr Chivers worked with Alfie, brushing his coat and putting a bucket of water in his stall, then disappeared to the sheds where the cows were kept. Their bellows subsided to a low mumble as he spoke to them soothingly.

By noon, Teddy's hands were red and sore with blisters where the scrubbing brush had chafed, and his trousers were wet and covered in splotches of muck and straw. When the church clock struck twelve, Mr Chivers looked at him with a sour expression and said; 'Don't be late tomorrow.'

'No sir,' Teddy said. He ran most of the way home.

His father was sitting in his armchair by the fire, reading a library book. Teddy hoped he'd smile or congratulate him on his first day's paid work, but his father only scowled.

'You've made a real mess of those trousers,' he said. 'You ought to be more careful. Your mother's got enough to do without you making more washing for her.'

'I couldn't help it – I had to wash out the bottles and I got splashed...' But his father shook his head and returned his attention to his book.

His mother came into the living room and asked, 'How did it go?'

'Not bad,' Teddy said. 'He said I wasn't to be late tomorrow, so he wants me back. I couldn't get the horse to slow down, though, and Mum... he waters the milk down.'

'He does not,' his mother said. 'Creamiest milk in Bow, is Chivers'.'

'Don't you go spreading gossip about the man, he's your new employer and he won't stand for it.'

'He does,' Teddy said, uncertainly. 'He puts a bucket of water in for every bucket of milk.'

'Don't contradict your mother,' his father said, with an edge to his voice. Teddy nodded, and said, 'Yes sir.' To himself, he thought fiercely. 'He does, I saw it.'

Later, he told his sister.

'He watered the milk down, Jane!'

''Course he does,' she said, scornfully. 'They all do. Ain't you ever tasted proper milk before? Chivers just don't water it as much as the rest of them.'

'And he…'

After a couple of minutes, Jane asked, 'What?'

'He went into this house in Gladstone Road, with this woman…'

Teddy couldn't say any more. He felt odd, felt he needed to squirm a bit to get himself settled, couldn't look into his sister's eyes.

'Was it number 27?' she asked.

'Don't know… Third house from the Margaret Street end. The woman had ratty hair, sort of pale brown…'

'That's his sister.' Jane knew all the women in the local streets. 'Her husband died in the Great War. She's funny in the head, doesn't really know what year it is. Mum says Mr Chivers gives her half what he earns, otherwise she'd starve.'

They sat together in silence, thinking separate thoughts about war and work and death.

'Teddy,' Jane said. 'You wouldn't join this Spanish civil war malarkey, would you?'

Teddy didn't need to look at her to know that she was frightened. 'Spain's nothing to do with us,' he said. 'I'm not going to any foreign war, don't you fret.'

'Only, if you can't earn some money…' Jane was quiet for a few minutes. 'It's just… Dad isn't going to be able to work again unless his cough eases up, and I can't fetch in enough to keep us…'

Out of the workhouse, he thought. Where Aunt Marie had gone just before she died. He felt cold at the thought of his family following her through those filthy grey doors, but the thought of his new employment settled him.

'Mr Chivers wants me in again tomorrow,' Teddy said, reassuring himself more than Jane. 'He wants me to go on with it. I'll make loads of money, you'll see. You can go back to school on what I earn.'

'Not going back to school however much you earn, thank you!' Jane said firmly, and they both laughed, quietly enough that their mother didn't hear them.

That night, Teddy dreamed of Betty Boop swimming in a pool of milk and woke to his mother's gentle touch on his shoulder at dawn.

## The Seagull

*Mairibeth MacMillan*

Seagull on the rocks
looking proud, majestic, white.
Looking for dead meat.

## The Spider that Eats the Soup

*Enza Vynn-Cara*

That very first time, in anger, I threw the potato soup at my older sister and then, like a spider, crawled under the table, fearful of my mother. I was more hungry than angry, and whining, I asked for more. She said there would be no soup for me yet filled my sister's bowl a second time. They sat and ate and laughed while I crawled further into myself, listening to the slurping and smacking of my sister's lips and her mouth-filled voice taunting me, 'It's good — so good.'

That night, I dreamed of the spider that eats its mate, slurping and smacking until nothing is left. In the morning, I was soaked red and my sister did not wake. Her mouth was smeared with soup; the smell of it still hung in the air. She was buried two days later, in her Sunday dress with the squared buttons running down the middle, and the blue shoes she hardly ever wore. My mother never made potato soup again. But I still crave it, at dusk and at dawn, when hunger pangs strike, most painfully, and I dream of the spider that eats its mate.

'It's a dream that soaks me red each time I eat the damn potato soup…'

I don't get to finish what I wanted to say. My face slams on Jake's Pub counter and meteorites skirt around the smoke filled room.

'Hope the bump got you sober.' The Hong Kong girl stares down at me with an eyebrow raised in surprise and a smirk of disbelief on her lips.

'It's all true.' I say, reaching for the beer. How many had I had so far? Enough, I hope, to stop the potato soup from haunting me tonight. 'I haven't eaten any since that day, you know, because of the spider that eats the soup and then its mate.'

'Oh yes, the spider that eats its mate.' She shrugs her bare shoulders and pouts her china-doll lips. 'Perhaps,' she says through a twitch of a smile, 'you should try my potato soup. I'm a great cook and my kitchen is clean, no spiders there.'

She scribbles a number on a napkin, buries it inside my shirt pocket, then walks away with her head turned so I can still catch her gaze out of the corner of her eye.

I think about her every night. I know I want her, with or without the potato soup. It's been a while. On Friday, we meet again in the same pub. I sit close to her and say, 'perhaps you should prepare the soup for me, just the way my mother did: one onion, two cloves of garlic, black pepper, parsley, and lots of new potatoes. And then perhaps the spider won't eat its mate.'

'Tomorrow, say...' She taps the empty wine glass with her lilac nails. 'Around seven-thirty? It's 18 Saddle Brook Road.'

I know she likes flowers, so I send her roses by special delivery and bring some Chilean red wine. Her studio flat is minimalist and cosy: a full moon Chinese lamp hangs down from a blue ceiling and in one corner, behind a see-through bamboo bookcase, a sofa bed is set out for the night. The lilac sheets and satin pillows tempt me. I force my gaze on her child-like stare, which doesn't blink but holds mine steady.

'You look good,' she says, relieving me of the bottle of wine.

I brush her cheeks with my lips.

She smells of oriental spices behind the ears.

'Mmm,' I say, 'I am hungry.'

'Right this way.'

She leads me into the alcove she calls a kitchen. It's a tiny stretch of a rectangle with copper pots and pans hanging from a pegboard above the white backsplash. At the very end, a table is set for two. Lilac candles burn on either side of the bouquet of roses I sent her, the glassware sparkles, and the air is wild with the smell of potato soup. I sit at one end of the table. She hands me the wine and sits on the other side, drawing toward her the glass bowl out of which swirl plumes of steam.

'The way your mother made it.'

She lists the ingredients one by one, tenderly stirring the mixture. I think she's pretty and petite and I eat the soup offered to the last spoonful, slurping and smacking my lips with delight. She's really a good cook. We make love. The satin sheets feel cool, her body much too warm, and then we sleep. When at dawn I awake, she's lying next to me smiling with mischief.

'See, there is no spider that eats its mate.'

I smile too. This petite thing might be right, I think, but then I hear the slurp the spider makes and smell the potato soup that killed my sister.

I'm hungry.

## Through a Glass Darkly

*Mairibeth MacMillan*

Lurking in my thoughts,
shadows form
just out of reach.
Ungraspable, half-formed doubts
that hinder hopes
and disturb my dreams.
Darkness drapes my outlook,
with a deadening curtain of futility,
which spreads,
tainting all that it touches.
Pleasant thoughts have
the darkest shadows.
Black flames
lick and curl
around their edges,
destroying any
brightness that they touch,
smothering joy
with hopelessness.
While I struggle to understand which is real.
Although sometimes the shadows
fade — my thoughts
remain bleak;
tinted by a shadowed lens
I want to clear.

I try to think
through that dark glass
but no glimmer of light
can penetrate
to distinguish the real
from the sickness.

## Tunnels of Love

*Sue Cook*

Remember when the earth first moved for us?
With open eyes I watched you heave below
before the compost bins your gradely show
convinced me we would be forever thus.
In search of mouthfuls moist you ploughed my beds,
devoured my demons, gorged with single mind
and in your wake you left no pest behind
resulting in such shiny, plump courgettes.
Of course it could not last and, undermined,
my world collapsed, gave way, I fell to earth,
a painful break both shocking and abrupt.
Now still I watch you leave me so, so blind
make crazy loop-the-loops beneath the birch,
my ankle and my lawn completely f*cked.

## Twenty-One Days

*Annis Farnell*

Twenty-one days. Three weeks. That is all the time I have to live. It is strange, to know in advance the day of my death; nor yet the day only, but the hour, the very minute, at which life shall be snuffed out. Some might deem it a privilege to know, to have the opportunity to make ready. I can only think of all that I shall miss: not the great events, but the small, daily happenings that constitute a life — the first sight of tender green in spring, the warmth of a summer breeze, even the icy kiss of winter in this cold city, with its views of the broad firth and the hills beyond.

I feel no different: my appetite, always hearty, is undiminished, my mind is clear and I suffer no bodily ills. And yet, and yet … in three short weeks I shall die, the constant care that I am given a continual reminder. Within I am still the same woman who sailed for the Crimea with Miss Nightingale, the same girl who, too plain and poorly-dowered to marry, was reared for the purpose of caring for her parents in their dotage, repaying their generosity in rearing me with lifelong duty.

Duty! Hateful word, redolent of unpleasant burdens unwillingly shouldered, but the lodestar of my life, until that Fateful day, when I gathered my courage, and told them I was leaving.

'I forbid it,' said Father, at his most uncompromisingly stern. 'It is your duty to remain here.'

He started to enumerate all that he and Mama had done for me, but I interrupted him, for the first time ever; I think it was surprise that silenced him.

'I am of age, Father,' I pointed out. 'And there is a higher duty calling me, to serve and to succour our poor soldiers.'

Not only was I of age: my grandmother had recently died, and had left me money — no great sum, a matter of some hundred pounds a year, but enough to secure my independence; and he knew it. He blustered, but bolstered by the example of Miss Nightingale herself, I stood firm, and in the end, he had perforce to let me go.

The lofty trumpet calls of duty and service, and the drum-roll summons of adventure faded to stillness in the face of what we found in the Crimea. There is no need to tell it here again, so much having been written of it already; suffice to say that it was there, in Scutari, that I met him, my friend, my love, my foe, my Nemesis.

When they brought him into the hospital, he seemed quite cheerful, and free from pain, which should have told me instantly the extent of his injuries, for one leg had its shattered bones roughly splinted and bandaged, and by rights, he should have suffered the most hideous agonies; but it was only when he was examined, and it was found that he had neither feeling nor movement below the waist, that it was realised that the leg (which was amputated, with him joking the while in that blackly courageous way men adopt when they are terrified) was a relatively minor injury. His back was broken, and some said he was lucky to have survived at all. His comrades, more prosaic, remarked that he had been better off dead.

He himself remained obstinately cheerful, no doubt buoyed up by the false hope so foolishly offered him by a doubtless well-meaning doctor, who told him that some cases of paralysis healed in time, and the sufferers walked again. I saw no self-deception, only what I took to be a splendid courage that outfaced the prospect of life as a cripple; saw too, the boyish charm that endeared him to all. I saw a man who found me attractive, and paid me small compliments whose sincerity I might trust, and not the lavish flattery that even such a simpleton as I might have found suspect.

The days are running out rapidly; as each dawn lights my narrow window, I count one less. I shall be thirty-five years and six days old when I die, so I shall receive no wishes for 'many happy returns'. But there, it has been some years since any wished me happy on my natal day.

As he grew stronger, he made overtures of such friendship as is deemed respectable, though it surprised me that I should be their object. I am not unduly modest: I am better educated than most women, to the extent of being feared a blue-stocking, and I flatter myself that I can converse intelligently with any, but our stations in life were so far removed, he the youngest son of a Viscount, I the daughter of merchant stock. A friendship between us was therefore, a matter for some wonder, and not confined to me, for my sister nurses, even Miss Nightingale herself, remarked on it. Remarked, and warned me.

The snow is falling thickly outside, so that I must have a lamp lit. How I should love to don boots and cloak, and walk in it! And come in with feet and fingers frozen, my hair and garments sodden with its melt. Perhaps I want it, because it is something I will never enjoy again.

I should, of course, have heeded the warnings, but my feelings for him were rapidly becoming warmer than mere friendship, and I closed my ears to wiser counsel. Had I been more versed in the ways of the world, I might have wondered why a gentleman such as he should have been a mere trooper, and not an officer, but I had never heard the term, 'gentleman ranker', and had no concept of what it stood for. It was with delight that I learned that he loved me too, and I accepted his proposal of marriage.

I find I am sleeping less well. It is a full moon tonight, and its light, reflecting off the snow, is making night almost as bright as day. Perhaps it is that which keeps me wakeful, rather than thoughts of eternity. I have a bible, but I ceased to read it many years ago; its comfort is not for me. Wherever I shall be in ten days' time, it cannot be worse than where I have been.

We were married in Scutari, and I was discharged from my duties as he was discharged from his bed, and we set out on the long journey back. On the ship, he exerted himself to be charming to me and to others, and despite his condition, to remain cheerful and full of hope.

We came here, to this place where we were unknown — it occurred to me to wonder why he did not take me to his father's house, but he told me it was to safeguard his independence from his well-meaning but smothering family; and I, poor fool, whose one goal had been freedom from the bonds of family, I believed him!

We found a small lodging, at ground level, with a tiny patch of garden where he might take the air in his wheeled chair, and with my annuity and his small pension, I thought we might go on tolerably well, but he apostrophised our lifestyle as shabby-genteel.

We also found a doctor, whose ethics were less elastic than those of his predecessor, and who had no belief in the benefits of false hope. My husband had no alternative but to accustom himself to his condition, and make the best of it. Making the best of things was not his forte; I returned from shopping next morning to find him gone. Four hours later, when I was at my wits' end with worry, he reappeared, exceedingly well to live and raucously singing bawdy songs, his chair being manhandled over the cobbles by a coarse lout in almost as bad a state.

From drinking, he went to gambling. His losses made him even more vile-tempered, and he drank even more. I grew accustomed to cleaning him, and tolerating the foul abuse he would hurl at me when in his cups. But his debts mounted, and rapidly outran our slender means. I believe he wrote to his family, but as I never saw the reply, I collect they preferred their black sheep and his wife to starve in the slum to which we had, perforce, to move.

This is my birthday, my last birthday. To my surprise, my carers have brought me a small cake to have with my tea, and a volume of poetry. They have been strangely kind to me, almost as though they sympathise. Perhaps they do. At any rate, this small act of generosity has brought me to the tears I had thought never to shed again.

Our life together, never, since those early days, a matter for joy, degenerated slowly into a hell — for both of us, I think, though I was the one who more obviously suffered. Sober, he was vituperative, vitriolic and hateful; drunk (which he was more and more often) he was violent and cruel. Fate might have robbed him of his lower limbs, but as if in compensation, his arms became exceedingly powerful through wrestling to propel his chair; and he could still throw things with remarkable accuracy. Indeed, he boasted once with no little satisfaction, having felled me with a bottle flung across the room, he had excelled in sports that required a strong arm and a good aim. And still I had to go to him, to be close to him, to perform all the necessary tasks of caring for him.

And still he could charm me, convince me that he would reform, but his fits of remorse rarely lasted longer than it took him to find the price of another bottle; even so, I stood his bullying, beatings and petty cruelties for twelve years. The lessons took time to learn, but in time I mastered them: first I learned to fear him; then I learned to hate. And out of that hate grew a passion stronger than I have ever known, whose sole end was to see his. I have had twenty-one days of dying, and my end will be swifter and less painful than his. I have no regrets; he was a brute, and deserved to die.

There is no reprieve, it seems; but I had hardly expected one. I have eaten my last meal, a piece of chicken, poached, with a trifle to follow. I can hear feet approaching: the chaplain, to help me make my peace with God. I kneel obediently, but do not listen; why should I compound with a Being (if He exists at all) who has never shown me any care? I am not afraid to die.

The minister's mumblings cease, and I stand. The doors of my cell – not the one the minister entered by, but the others, the twin doors that have remained closed for the three weeks I have been here – the doors open, to admit a party of men. Over their heads, I can see into the room beyond, and see the instrument of my death. I am not afraid.

I bid the wardresses, those almost kindly, constant companions of my last days, a brief farewell, and then my arms are bound. I am not afraid.

They take up station before and behind me, and we move forward in the last few steps I shall ever take. I am not afraid.

The hood is pulled over my unresisting head, and if I cast my eyes downward, I can see beneath its rim the outline of the trap through which I must descend so abruptly into night. My view is cut off as, snake-like, the rope settles heavily round my neck. I can feel hands adjusting it, so that it fits close under my chin, the thicker part, where they have tied the knot, under my left ear. I am not afraid.

*I am not afraid.*

*I AM NOT -*

## Untitled

*Elves*

I always knew that joining wouldn't be easy; that the threat of being blackballed would hang over me. So I'd been surprised to get as far as this test. If I could pass this, well then would come the vote of all the members to see if they would let me in. But the test was important and all I had to do was arrange for the eight of us to visit the island for the weekend. Pat was the most likely to blackball me, and most of the others followed his lead, so I had to make sure that he in particular had a good time, something he would remember, something he would put down to me. Perhaps then, when the vote came, Billy could persuade him, at the very worst, just to abstain.

Andy was driving the car I was in, not slowly as the road demanded, but with tyres squealing as he forced the thing around the last of the right-angled bends, then accelerating hard along the straight section that led directly to the sands and the causeway over to the island.

Having gotten used to that, I wasn't expecting suddenly and without warning to be flung forward, where I came into collision with the front seat. What had fooled me was that, from the experience of the drive north, I had come to believe that the car wasn't fitted with brakes, so it was a bit of a surprise to find out not only that my belief was wrong, but also that they were fully functional. And now Andy had his foot hard down on that previously unsuspected middle pedal. I tried to push myself back into my seat, gave up the attempt in the face of the deceleration, and waited until the suddenness of the stop, an instant or so later, pushed me back without any effort on my part.

'Christ, Andy.' It was Billy who said that, almost yelled, from the seat beside mine. Meanwhile, I tried to regain my bearings. There had been no loud bang, which would have indicated that we'd crashed, and outside, the first thing I saw was the other car, parked on the grass at the side of the road, with its occupants – all four of them – huddled around some sort of notice board at the far side of the car. They were shouting – at what wasn't immediately obvious – and jabbing fingers at some sort of notice affixed to the board.

The next thing I saw was what had forced Andy to put his anchors down. The tide was in!

The causeway, a thin ribbon of asphalt that was supposed to carry us across to the island, could only be seen by virtue of two little parallel lines of foam, marking the places where the water came onto the road and then cascaded off it. The slightly raised road surface was only vaguely visible under the water.

'Fuck, fuck, fuckity fuck,' said Leonard, sitting in his front seat vantage point and summing up our situation rather succinctly.

I felt my heart miss a beat. I screwed up my eyes then opened them again, hoping that the view might have changed. It hadn't. The ocean was still there, where it had no business to be. My test was not going well. Without realising it, I was already rehearsing in my head the inevitable confrontation with Pat. It was a simple test he had laid down – get us all across to the island for a drunken weekend. How hard could that be? Well, as Andy and Leonard both turned to look at me, I returned their glances with a little laugh and thought that, at least for me, the test had turned out to be too hard. I tried to swallow but my throat felt very thick and extraordinarily dry. I wished – oh how I wished – that I wasn't sitting there at that moment.

'I thought you'd fucking organised this,' Andy accused.

'Did you think to check the fucking tide charts,' Leonard added.

Of course I had.

'And did you check that it was this fucking week's fucking tide charts?'

That slight amendment to Leonard's question created a new doubt in my mind. Could I possibly have checked the wrong charts? I could remember reading them in the library. But were they the right ones?

'Fucking hell, John,' said Billy, my sponsor, and the only one I could really rely on. He would always be on my side. 'Pat'll go ballistic.'

'I think you might be right there,' said Andy. 'He's looking this way. And … oh Christ … he's got that look on his face. Arms folded. Legs spread. Tapping his feet. I've seen that look before.'

'And I think we'd better get out and get over there and look at those charts for ourselves.' Billy, the voice of reason. Billy, my friend. 'Let's see how long we're going to be stranded here.'

'Instead of being in the pub,' Leonard added.

So the recriminations had started, and we weren't even out of the car. They hadn't needed Pat either. They were quite able to get stuck into me on their own account. They got out of the car. I got out last of all. And I followed them to the notice board, hands in pockets, shuffling, shoulders sagging — I could feel them sagging. This was the long walk of the condemned man.

'What the fuck were you pillocks thinking?' Pat demanded. 'Proposing a fucking arsehole like that.' His forefinger jabbed at the air in my direction. 'Organise an outing? He couldn't organise a piss up in a brewery. Couldn't get the fucking time of his own fucking funeral right.'

Amongst all the various denials that filled the air, he took a step towards me. Only Billy stepped in his way; put his hand on Pat's shoulder.

'Take it easy Pat,' he suggested, more, I thought, in hope than expectation.

'Take it fucking easy?' Pat shouted, and his eyes never left my face. 'Take it fucking easy? We should be over there now,' and he turned his head and pointed at the island, then just as quickly jerked it back in my direction.

I had certainly succeeded in my objective: I had made it really memorable for him. He wouldn't forget this in a hurry.

The remaining three of the group had all left the tide chart to its own devices while all of this greeting between old friends was going down. Now they stood, ranged beside Pat, looking at me. I thought of the scene in the film about the gunfight at the OK Corral, or at least I did as long as my friends stood beside me. But that didn't last long. Andy changed position first, turning to face me directly and standing right beside Pat. Leonard joined him, and then Billy went over to study the tide chart for himself, leaving me stranded and awaiting the pleasure of the firing squad. I was left to get on with it. Alone. In the dock. The accused. And there couldn't be the slightest doubt about the verdict. No need for evidence.

'Well I'm not hanging around here like a stale fart,' said Pat. 'I'm going across. How deep can it be?'

There was a murmur of agreement. Pete said he would wait and bring the car over when the causeway was clear. Andy agreed, a touch reluctant I thought.

'And you're fucking coming over with me,' said Pat, now jabbing that forefinger of his directly into my shoulder.

'What about the current?' I said. 'It's not …'

'Never mind about the fucking current,' he shouted, his face so close to mine that I could feel his hot breath bathe me. 'The current doesn't fucking matter, as we'll have someone in front, checking it out for the rest of us.'

I didn't doubt who that lucky person might be.

'I'll buy the first round when we get …'

'I wouldn't fucking touch a fucking pint that you fucking bought,' he interjected, 'you fucking wanker.'

I turned my back on him and walked back to the road. There seemed little point in trying to change his attitude. He was going to veto me and he wouldn't be the only one. There was no longer anything I could do about it.

I thought about taking off my sandals to keep them dry, but then I thought that walking along a tarmacked road with bare feet wouldn't be a great laugh either. So I contented myself with taking off just my socks and then rolling up my trousers to the knees. The water was likely only about six inches deep. There was no point getting my clothes wet.

I took my first steps into the sea, and to my surprise I found it rather easy. For the first few yards the water didn't even cover my feet. But by the time I approached the halfway marker it was a rather different story. It was more like a foot deep there, and there was a strong current. It created what I think is called a bow shock wave, which meant that the left hand sides of my legs were in water that only came up to my ankles, but the waves at the right hand sides reached well up my thighs. My trousers were soaking and my shirt was getting wet too, as the lads behind me were splashing me, making fun of me, making a lot of noise. 'Just put up with it,' I thought. 'Just put up with it.'

I reached the halfway marker without pausing. Here the causeway crossed the main drainage channel. When the tide went out, this stretch would be the last to show its sandy bottom. Now I was getting seriously wet as more and more water was thrown at me. Pat of course. Leading the opposition. But I could hear Billy's voice too. He had lost face as the one who had sponsored me, and now he had to prove that he was still one of the gang. He wanted to impress Pat.

That's what made it so much worse. I'd been friends with Billy from years back. Best mates at school, we'd gone our separate ways until we met up a few months ago.

I wasn't expecting it when someone punched me on the top of my right arm. I flinched, which was a shame, because it meant that I lost my balance. That was when I felt the real force of running water. I clawed at the air — but you can't hang on to that — and felt my body succumb to gravity and fall. That was more than just a shame, because I didn't fall onto the causeway, but into the deeper water of the channel. My feet couldn't find the bottom and the current just carried me off. I could hear them laughing, somewhere off in the distance, receding. They evidently found it very funny to see me soaked. I gulped in huge mouthfuls of seawater, waved my arms around as I flailed helplessly and tried to swim, without any success. I never was a very strong swimmer — only learned since I left school — and I didn't have a frequent visitor card at the local swimming pool. I had always thought that bodies were supposed to float, but that didn't seem to be the case with mine. Perhaps I had swallowed too much when I fell in. Every time I tried to breath all I got was another mouthful of water — or was that a lung full. Coughing was an automatic reaction, but it didn't help either.

I was only twenty-one years old, with my whole life ahead of me, yet suddenly, the prospect of a twenty second birthday party seemed to be receding. Oddly though, I didn't panic. I stopped flailing, tried to save my strength, and felt strangely peaceful. The prospect of the black ball didn't seem to be so very important now.

I don't know how I got out of the water, or even where I was, I just can't remember, but I knew I was back on land because everything was light and bright, in stark contrast to the water. I looked up and saw that I was on the beach, and my parents were there, waiting for me. Something told me that that was odd, since I hadn't seen either of them for over four years, not since the accident on the M6. There was someone else too, standing with them. I knew him, but couldn't quite place him, but he exuded friendship — in fact it was a feeling of love such as I had never experienced before — and I was no longer afraid; no longer burning with a sense of injustice at my treatment at the hands of my friends, or with the humiliation of having looked up the wrong dates on the tide charts. There was just peace and a deep sense of love and joy in the air around me.

Now, I know it's a cliché, but I really don't have words of my own to describe what happened next. The stranger – I'll call him that even though I was sure that I knew him – he spoke to me; and as he did my whole life flashed before my eyes. It wasn't so difficult, since I'd done nothing exceptional and always thought that I'd have enough time later to do loads of great things. But I could see clearly everyone I'd ever met, and relive what I'd said and done, all those little things that I'd carried on my conscience for a day or so, until something new took them out of my mind. Now I could feel everything again, as surely as when they happened the first time around.

The stranger told me that it wasn't really my time. I knew what he meant, but I felt so disappointed. It was the very last thing I wanted to do. I would prefer to stay where I was, with mum and dad, but how could I? It wasn't my time. Hadn't he just told me so?

I was coughing my lungs up, on a sandy beach. Someone was doing something to me, using a lot of force. Was he kissing me? I opened my eyes. It was Pat, and he was sitting on top of me, or rather, astride me. I tried to push him off, totally ineffectually I have to say.

'You stupid prat,' he said, before he climbed off me and in one movement turned me over. The coughing redoubled and what was left of the seawater in my lungs spewed out onto the sand.

I don't know how long I lay there, only that when I finally felt able to move, I was alone with Pat. The others had crossed over except for one car that was moving carefully across the causeway, now that the water level had dropped. He helped me to my feet, thumped me on the back a couple of times to help me cough up any remaining water, then asked if I was ok.

I looked at him with a mixture of surprise and peacefulness and noticed, for the first time, the vague shimmer of light about his head. 'Thank you,' I said. Then I noticed that, like me, he was soaked to the skin. 'It was you?' I asked. 'You pulled me out?'

'Couldn't let you drown could I,' he answered. 'That would have really fucked up the whole weekend.'

And when I said nothing in return he added, 'Listen John. The test isn't about whether you can arrange a weekend away. It's about how well you get on with all of us. You might have fucked up the tides, but it's not the first time someone's done that. And last time I looked, no one had ever been put to death for it.'

'I just don't know what happened,' I said.

'That fucking Billy shoved you in,' Pat said. 'Stupid prat. He could've killed you.'

'I think he did,' I replied, at which Pat stopped walking and turned to look at me. I looked back at him. 'I think I died and went to heaven,' I said.

He was still looking at me, a hard stare, then he began to nod slowly and a smile crept over his face. I had the oddest feeling that the shimmering light about him, which was fading, sparkled again.

'Did you go down the tunnel?' he asked, and by way of reply I nodded.

'And did you get to the other side? Did you see them?'

I nodded again. We were both standing perfectly still, perfectly in accord.

'And they sent you back?'

'I'm not sure I wanted to come back.'

'They can be persuasive though, eh?'

'Have you been there Pat? Have you seen it too?'

'Welcome to the club,' he said. He didn't spell out which club he meant, but somehow that didn't matter. Not any more.

## Victor

*RJ Ashby*

On the bear's side a tiny label sewn tight reads "Victor by Mme T".

How odd for me, an old woman now, to say that Victor is my companion. I don't remember where he came from. He has a presence, a tangible presence, my dearest... Someone sent him to keep me safe – a Turkish or Hungarian connection. You know, one of those family legends.

Emotions stir to alter the steps of memory. It's a long time since I lived a beaming childhood. I can see it still: the front door, black and gleaming, polished and unblemished, a match to my innocence. The brass handle filled my two hands as I made efforts to escape. And then I would sit grandly on the cool stone steps above the city street: fresh with excitement. At times I had been allowed to sit. I remember Grandmamma coming, and sometimes a stranger. We took tea in the lounge.

Victor came from those distant times. When my world was facing forwards and the sun shone bright and my mother held my hand.

Even now, a cloud marks my brow; my stomach turns and I look for Victor. That brutal day my sheltered shell smashed. I stood alone. I stood in black. My tiny frame clutched Victor and he hummed and lulled me through the days of pain.

My mother was gone. Victor's era began.

Victor, in his golden mohair skin, was there. His head sat at just that angle of concern: an ear to my whispered fears. His eyes spoke. My embrace felt full. He would calm and cool, caress and cure — my constant across the years, and there have been many years.

Now it's time.

I'm done. The reaper beckons. Today I've been for a last meander around a gallery. Fatigue has drawn me to the café.

I sit. My bag has fallen over and there is Victor lying with his eyes set clearly across the aisle. I follow his gaze. A little girl, pale and listless, sits so still. As I watch, she lays her head down on the table and I see. I see that she has seen my bear. Her face warms, relaxes. And she watches. I cast a casual glance at her companion who is reading. I watch Victor. I can see him if I look from the menu and focus on the floor. He is winning with his selfless care on the cold stone floor. I let him lie. Is this goodbye?

Only Victor knows. I bend down and gently lift him. I ask him. I feel him tense. His eyes brighten.

'Can you look after Victor for me? I'm going to the Ladies.'

I return and know.

'Would you like to look after him?'

'Oh she can't do that!' Her carer spoke.

'Well, I'm moving soon. I was taking him to a charity shop. You can save me that trouble. What do you say?'

I look carefully at the little girl who whispers, 'Yes please.' as she hugs him tight.

*James More, a friend, wrote his own wonderful story about Mme T who was an ageing eastern lady who sat in her rocking chair and sewed her love into the fabric of special teddy bears. The toys were filled with understanding and love and they found children who were victims and they protected them.*

*James died from cancer in 2011.*

## What I know

*Enza Vynn-Cara*

There are days
when I think I'm drunk
then there are days when I know you are.
That sort of day I cling to my antidepressant.

Then I see,
I see through the eye of sobriety
and for an instant
all feels right — feels real:

your socks, finally
inside their rightful drawer,
each morning
our booted daily walk across
the thicket at the back of our home,
and in the evening
in the shade by the pond with the red and white fishes,

we sit and talk
about the things that never happen,
the walks that grow too short
and the socks you can never find.

And when we laugh

and laugh
and laugh again – into the night –
our lips moistened by early dew and malt flavoured ice cubes,

I forget.

I forget why you drink,
why you don't want me anymore,
why I drink, too.

That sort of day I know, I know that I'm as drunk as you.

## When We Were Nine

*Palo Stickland*

Anna knew where to grip with her fingers, knew to place her foot on the brick bin shelter for support before pulling herself on to the wall that separated the two back gardens of the Glasgow tenements. It was a stone wall about twice her height but when she sat astride it the other side was only about as tall as she was, which was medium for a nine-year-old. Tanveer must be around back of the air-raid shelter which took up most of the space that was the 'garden' for eight families, and more, when you included the lodgers.

Anna remembered her father saying, 'The war has been over for nearly fifteen years and these air-raid shelters are still taking up space. Perhaps they're waiting for the next one.'

She could imagine all those people running into it in the middle of the night with the sirens warning of enemy planes overhead. They would sit inside waiting for the 'all clear'. Anna's mum had told her about it.

The sound of the little ones was closer now. She had waved and called to Tanveer from her window, racing down as soon as she saw them out, but she knew her friend would not see her.

She was short-sighted but wouldn't wear her glasses outside of the class, said her mum didn't like them.

Here she was now coming around the shelter with her brothers tumbling along behind her. She laughed and shouted 'Hello, Anna!'

'Isn't it great to be on school holidays, Tanveer? I was visiting my granny in Fife.'

'Did you have a good time?'

'Yes.' Anna said, 'I waved from the window but you didn't see me.'

Tanveer looked up towards the third-floor windows of the tenement opposite and Anna wondered if she was thinking about how empty her house was compared to her own. Tanveer's mother slept on the folding bed-settee in the kitchen with her three little brothers. Her father's bed was in the alcove and she, Tanveer, being the only girl, was allowed the tiny room off the kitchen. They also had two elderly lodgers in one room whereas Anna was an only child with her mum and dad in a huge flat.

All these images flitted across Anna's mind as she jumped off the wall, but now stopped still, pointing at the ground, where the wind had blown the overflowing rubbish from the bins, 'Oh Tanveer, that's your prize book! Mrs Hammond gave it to you only two weeks ago. It's torn!'

Tanveer looked sadly at the rubbish. 'It's 'Smuggler Ben' by Enid Blyton. I've read it.'

Anna looked horrified as Tanveer turned away to tend to her little brother.

## Whipped Cream and Marshmallows

*Mairibeth MacMillan*

'Celebrating?' I sipped my hot chocolate envious of Sarah's which was topped with whipped cream and a layer of gooey, melting marshmallows.

'What, oh, the toppings? No... Yes... Sort of... I met someone.'

'A guy someone?'

'Yeah,' Sarah giggled and it was the first time I'd heard her giggle since... since the last break-up.

'And?'

'I met him at the office party last night,' Sarah said. My spoon clattered onto the saucer.

'I thought you'd decided that men from work were off limits after David.'

'He's not from my work – his work were just having their night out in the Grosvenor at the same time – must be Fate.'

I laughed. Every man Sarah met was led to her by Fate. If Fate had lined such a collection of losers up for me I'd have told Fate not to bother.

'He's a doctor, at the Western,' Sarah added.

'Really?' At least Fate had found someone with a stable job for once.

'A heart surgeon.' Sarah gushed. I hadn't seen her smile so brightly in years. Maybe this time Fate was onto a winner. Then I looked at Sarah's mug and wondered how Dr Wonderful would view the enormous cup of sugar and cholesterol that Sarah was drinking.

'What?' she asked.

'Nothing,' I said and shifted my gaze to her face. 'So, tell me all about him.'

'Everything okay?' the waiter interrupted before Sarah could get started.

'Fine, thanks,' I said at the same time as Sarah said 'Great.' If I'd had her drink I'd have said 'great' too.

'Can I get you anything else?' he offered and I looked up. Usually you had to go to the counter to get anything.

'Another hot chocolate, thanks.' I hoped he wouldn't get in trouble bringing drinks to the table then I caught sight of his badge. *Gregor MacDonald, Manager.*

'Nothing for me, thanks,' said Sarah. 'I have to run. Need to catch the dry-cleaners. I'll see you next month, okay?'

'Sure,' I said but she was gone so fast I doubt she heard me. When my hot chocolate arrived it had cream and marshmallows on it.

The café was quiet so it also came with company.

The following month Sarah and I were due to meet on Burns Night. By the time she finally arrived I had almost had enough of the café's incessant bagpipe music.

'Sorry, sorry,' she gushed, stuffing an enormous pile of bags under the seat.

'*House of Fraser*?'

'So?' she sounded defensive.

'So, that's a lot of bags from the *House of Fraser*. Especially all at once.'

'Martin wanted me to pick some things up for him. And he wanted me to get something more suitable to wear for the wedding we're going to.'

'More suitable?'

'Oh, don't be like that. It's just he felt that the things I had weren't quite right for the sort of wedding we're going to.'

I said nothing.

'You're just jealous because you're single,' Sarah snapped. Gregor approached and we smiled at each other.

'Hot chocolate?'

'A latte for me, please,' Sarah said. 'Martin thinks I should cut down on my sugar intake.'

No surprise there, then. I watched Gregor at the counter making the two drinks. He winked over at me when I saw him put extra marshmallows in mine. Sarah didn't stay long but I did.

I'd come to the café on Valentine's Day even though it wasn't the week I was due to meet Sarah. I'd had a really nice afternoon. There had been a Valentine on the tray beside my hot chocolate and I had left one with my tip.

Today was spoiling that memory. Sarah arrived late, again, and dumped a pile of prospectuses on the table.

'What's up?' I started to ask but was distracted by the appearance of Gregor.

'The usual?' he asked. I nodded.

'Green tea, please,' Sarah said not even taking the time to look at Gregor.

'Tea? You never drink tea. Especially green stuff,' I said, annoyed that she was ignoring him.

'Yes, I do.'

I sighed.

'I do so.' She picked up a prospectus and started to flick through it. 'Besides, Martin feels that I should cut down on my fat intake and he thinks caffeine makes me irritable.'

'Is he sure it's the caffeine that's making you irritable?' I couldn't help it. Sarah's relationships always followed the same path. Why could she not see it and get out before she got hurt?

'Of course he is,' she said shrilly. 'He's a doctor, he knows what he's talking about. You probably should think about cutting out all the sugar and fat in that hot chocolate you're always drinking.' There was silence for a while. Sometimes I found it hard to remember why we were friends.

'So,' I said just to break the silence. 'How was the wedding?'

'Fine,' she snapped back.

'Just fine? No, "the bride looked lovely?" Or "the bridesmaid's dresses were hideous." Just fine?'

'I don't know what you expect me to say, Becca. The wedding was very tasteful and the dresses were very pretty. It was one of Martin's closest friends so, of course, everything was *au courant*.'

I just laughed and asked, 'What's with all this?'

Sarah looked at the pile on the table and I could have sworn that there was a look of horror on her face.

'Martin feels that maybe I'm not pushing myself enough, you know, career-wise.'

'He could be right,' I replied cautiously. Sarah's job as a beautician was what she had always wanted to do and I knew she really enjoyed it. 'I always thought you should think about setting up your own salon.'

For a fleeting moment her eyes lit up then the light slowly extinguished.

'I don't think...' She paused. 'Actually, I was thinking about retraining.' The silence grew between us. 'There are a few possibilities... I could polish up my secretarial skills or perhaps think about training as a teacher, you know I've always liked children.'

'Since when?'

'I just think I should consider, you know, something a little more professional.'

'I thought you loved your job.'

'Martin doesn't think –'

'Sarah, it's your job, not Martin's. Are you giving him career advice?'

'Don't be ridiculous. How could someone like me give advice to someone like him?' She toppled the pile of prospectuses over in her haste to stand. Her face was a bright scarlet and I thought she was going to cry. 'He warned me that someone like you wouldn't understand.'

'He's never even met me.'

'He doesn't have to, does he? He was right. You want me just to settle for what I am instead of trying to be something better.'

'I'm not the one who's embarrassed by what you do.' I was shaking as I stood and crossed the café to stand at the counter beside Gregor. I didn't look back.

'She's gone,' he said covering my hand with his own and I felt the tears start to fall. He closed the café early that day and we went out for dinner.

The next month Sarah didn't show up. She didn't text or e-mail either. I'd like to say that I missed the allotted day as well – by now I'd started going to the café every week – but I knew fine well which day she should have been there. I missed her but she had made her choice and I had a life of my own to live.

That day my hot chocolate had a dusting of powdered chocolate on it in the shape of a love heart. Cheesy but sweet. Gregor sat with me when the place was quiet and we drank hot chocolate together. Quality assurance he called it but we both knew it was something more.

We were chatting about our plans for the weekend when a shadow fell across us. Sarah.

'I didn't think you'd keep coming here by yourself,' she said.

'I come here every week now,' I said. 'And if you cared enough to notice, I'm not by myself.' Sarah frowned and looked at Gregor in confusion. Her mouth formed an 'o' when realisation set in.

'Can I get you anything?' Gregor asked and I looked at Sarah.

'Hot chocolate, please,' she said and sat down.

'No coffee? No tea? No green tea?' I asked.

'No Martin,' she said and tears sprang to her eyes.

'I'll leave you to catch up,' Gregor said, running a hand over my hair and kissing me. 'See you at five, Becca.'

Gregor left us alone to sort things out and brought over the drinks a few minutes later. Both were topped with a generous helping of cream and marshmallows.

I nodded and watched him as he got back to work. I smiled to myself at the thought that he was as warm and sweet as the hot chocolate then chided myself for being so twee.

'He seems nice.'

'He is,' I said, but I kept my attention on Gregor.

'You were right.'

'I know.' I turned to face Sarah. 'And you did too.'

Sarah nodded. 'I did. I just never seem to meet the right kind of man.'

'Well… I have.'

I looked over at Gregor again, aware I was probably grinning like a fool.

'Meeting up here every month had become such a strain but he was my silver lining,' I said.

Sarah stared at me for a moment or two then turned to look at Gregor. Then her head dropped and for a while we sat in silence. I sipped at my hot chocolate waiting for her to speak.

'Becca,' Sarah said finally. 'I'm sorry I was your cloud.'

I nodded, pleased that she'd finally realised it.

'It'll be different next time,' she promised.

We raised our mugs to that, clinking them gently together so as not to spill the hot chocolate. Maybe it would even be true.

## Author bios

**Annis Farnell…**

lives with a husband and assortment of wildlife in a B-listed wreck with half an acre of garden. Has a degree in Earth Sciences and a Diploma in Creative Writing from the OU, and has had a wide variety of jobs, including time at sea and working as a labourer on a building site. Interests are getting back to peak fitness, German and Scottish folk music, and classical and military history. Collects Biggles books. Has written three novels and had articles published in the local press as well as a recipe in a magazine.

**Enza Vynn-Cara…**

loves to travel and to learn languages by direct immersion into the local culture. Spanish is her next project and Spain is in her sight. She has been there four times, and plans a few more trips come next year. A self-learner whose passion for writing has become a full-time event, she aims to complete a BA in English Literature and Creative Writing within the year. She has written one novel (now in the revision phase) and has a second one in progress. She's also an enthusiast of short-story writing and flash-fiction.

**Julia Chalkley...**
grew up in the East End of London. She gained a degree in Earth Sciences from the Open University as an antidote to her career as an accountant, and went on to take a Diploma in Creative Writing with the OU for fun. Currently lives in Essex with a husband, four cats, eight motorcycles and a lot of cider apple trees.

**Elves...**
went to the University of Sussex for a degree in Chemistry; then to the Open University to get a degree in Literature. He chose that as Literature was his worst subject at school, and thought it would be a stretch. It was, but it was fun. Despite the degree, he still can't write poetry to save his life – read 'A Glass, Half Empty' for confirmation of that. He is presently putting the finishing touches to a novel.

**Mairibeth MacMillan...**

taught for more than ten years before deciding that she had repaid any outstanding debt to society and opted for a career change. Writing allows her to spend more time with family and not having to brave the Scottish weather to get to work is an added advantage. She writes about whatever subject appeals most at that particular moment and is easily distracted by both research and shiny new ideas.

Mairibeth can be found on Facebook as Mairibeth MacMillan, Pinterest as mairibeth and Twitter as @MairibethM.

**Palo Stickland...**

is the author of a family saga called Finding Takri, published in 2012. Her aim is to begin a novel on the 1st of January each year. However, due to travelling the world commitments, she is a wee bit behind schedule.

You can find a reference to the novel at palostickland.com

**R Cohen…**
is a Brit abroad. Having swapped the Thames for the Rhine, she has left London behind and now lives with her husband and son in Basel, Switzerland. She can often be found with a pen in one hand and a cup of Darjeeling in the other.

Meet up with Rebecca at rebeccacohenwrites.wordpress.com

**Russet J Ashby…**
studied education at Edinburgh and with the OU. Now she writes from a garret somewhere in Scotland where words tumble out onto page after page. One day she says she will feel like a writer. Until then … she has one completed manuscript that is *out there* at the moment, a historical adventure, and she is working on a story about a modern day family with problems. She also writes short stories and poetry.

**Sue Cook...**

is a frustrated crime novelist. Frustrated by knowing nothing whatever about the police and handicapped by being pathologically law abiding. The early influence of Max Boyce ensures all her romances turn to farce. Under the rising gloom of repetitive rejection, however, she finally kept it serious enough to Sell Something. Her writing aim is to earn enough to persuade her accountant that it is not a hobby, Martin, and can we put her expenses against tax now?

You can see Sue's blog at optimisticscribe.wordpress.com
Sue is on Pinterest at ukpinterest.com/cook3230

10608298R00112

Printed in Great Britain
by Amazon.co.uk, Ltd.,
Marston Gate.